ANDREW AND GRACE
The Harper Trilogy – Book One

by

Paula Stevenson

I'm the luckiest man on this earth. You want to know why? I smile to myself while lying on my bed. Dozing and thinking about her... blowing raspberries on her belly, going for long walks, watching sunsets overlooking the water and sitting at our favourite spot underneath the Harbour Bridge.

Those are all the things that I loved doing with her and still do. We had an unusual beginning to our life together, but all that I know is that she is the one person who, quite simply... completes me.

www.charlefieldbooks.com

Andrew and Grace

The Harper Trilogy – Book One

First Edition - January 2024
Sydney, Australia

Copyright © 2024 - Paula Stevenson

authorofcats@yahoo.com.au

I dedicate this book

to

all those who have lost hope…

remember… there is someone out there for all of us…

Contents

PREFACE

All written content has been derived from an over-active imagination and is purely coincidental and utterly fictitious. Paula Stevenson wishes to thank all those who read each draft leading up to publishing.

Thank you also to those who assisted with the artwork and editing, namely Sean Smith and Peter Krockenberger.

Without you all, this story would never have made it this far.

My eternal thanks for your invaluable assistance in all things book-related.

PROLOGUE

ANDREW

I'm the luckiest man on this earth. You want to know why? I smile to myself while lying on my bed. Dozing and thinking about her... blowing raspberries on her belly, going for long walks around the waterfront, watching sunsets overlooking the water, sitting in our favourite spot underneath the Harbour Bridge.

Those are all the things that I loved doing with her and still do. We had an unusual beginning to our life together, but all that I know is that she is the one person who, quite simply... completes me.

I find myself looking into her eyes as I lay my soul bare. Her beautiful green eyes shine with the threat of tears. I hope they are tears of joy as I put my hands in her auburn hair and reach over to kiss her, and she returns the kiss, matching my need.

And I open my eyes to realise it was another dream. "Fuck, I don't even know who she is. I haven't met anyone, ever, with auburn hair except that girl."

I roll over in bed trying to think about other things and wish I could go back to sleep. I opted to go to a country Local Area Command when I finished at Goulburn Police Academy.

I miss my mother. I haven't seen her much since I came to Broken Hill. I remember when I graduated. My mother was in the stands and she told me she was so proud of me and she cried and said, "You're welcome to move back in when you've finished your tour of duty." It would probably be hard to settle into city life again once I finish at Broken Hill.

I remember before we graduated from Goulburn I was in the city. We were called to do barrier work for the first time as there was going to be a huge parade in the city for some football team. I don't follow that code. We were told they needed more reinforcements. There might be opposition team fans causing trouble, so they wanted us to just do the standard crowd control.

We would be going via coaches up to Town Hall and there we would line the streets in full uniform amongst our fellow officers who had graduated before us. We were not returning to Goulburn until late afternoon, so we had some free time for lunch after the parade had finished.

I remember standing with my back to a barrier and there was a young woman standing opposite me with auburn hair and green eyes. I smiled at her and she blushed and looked away from me and then the parade ended and the last float was going past us, and the next time I looked towards her she was gone.

The crowd was slowly dispersing. I scanned the crowd up and down the street, but… nothing.

My heart was heavy but the very moment I saw her it was lighter than air.

Ever since then I have put her face into my dreams. I remember saying to myself, almost in a panic, 'I have to find her again.'

I moved to the station entrance on her side of the street at the Town Hall and impatiently pushed people out of the way in the hope of finding her, and then… then what? I searched everywhere but it was like looking for a needle in a haystack.

I went through the railway station barriers and to the platform that would take me to my Mum's at St Peters and I waited. I turned to my left as the train rolled in and, sure as my heart skipping a beat, there she was and I followed her as the doors opened. I sat next to her and slowly moved my hand towards hers as she looked out the window.

I've never been this brazen before, but I just have to know if it is true.

I gently touch her little finger with mine and she instinctively moves it towards her side. I stretch my hand again, edging closer and closer. My face is going red. I break out in a sweat.

There, I'm holding her hand in mine and she turns around and looks at me, scared. She sees my uniform and looks down at our hands. I smile and she smiles back at me. Confused, she tilts her head to the right and is about to ask why.

I leaned in towards her and whispered in her ear, "I've found you at last." She looks at me, stunned and unsure. She tries to jerk her hand away but I hold it tighter and I lean into her again and this time I say, "I've dreamt of you. I can't explain it... but every night, there you are." She looks at me like I'm a stalker or some kind of sicko, but then she sees my earnest expression and something in my deep blue eyes, perhaps?

"You're serious. Why?" she asks timidly. "I've never ever met you before."

"I wish I knew, but I feel (oh this is going to sound like a pick-up line), I feel like I've known you forever, like we are kindred spirits or something..." I rub my thumb against her knuckles and she doesn't move her hand away.

We sit in a comfortable silence, just looking into each other's eyes. The train pulls into Erskineville and I very reluctantly let her go. I wish I could see her again. I don't even know her name. The train edges closer to St Peters.

As I leave the seat, I turn back to look at her and there is no one on the train but us. We are the only two people alive in this world and our hearts beat in time. The electricity I felt as I touched her hand is less intense now that I've walked away and I look into her eyes and she looks into mine with unsaid questions, and I smile at her and go.

I wish I'd given her my number. I kick myself for not remembering to do that, but when I was with her everything just seemed to be in slow motion. I thought I had all the time in the world with her but reality reared its intrusive head and I remembered I was due to have lunch with my mother before I headed back to Goulburn. I was way too early to meet my mother as she was working half the day in the city. I would just let myself inside and rest and then Mother and I would chat.

I was due back in the city at 4pm to get the coach back to Goulburn. As I walked to Mum's place I began to think of that girl again.

Would I ever see her again? I hoped so. Perhaps I'd see her in my dreams…

GRACE

I'm here in the city, this overcrowded and at times suffocating place, because I have to buy a formal dress, under duress. My mother told me I had to. My father gave me some money and I argued with them, saying that I wasn't going to go, but they insisted. I didn't have a date or anything. I was given strict instructions to not buy a black dress. I think my brother was told he had to be my date. Oh, how pathetic am I? Sigh.

I wandered the city streets alone. When I got to the Dymocks building, I went inside to the bridal shop and stared at the beautiful wedding dresses and bridesmaid dresses and the happy girls who had their lives before them. I was just standing there admiring a grey dress when a stately woman approached me and looked me up and down and said, "Child, that dress is not your colour. How about the red one or this lovely green one? What's the occasion?"

I stutter that it's my Year Ten formal.

"Buy the green one, it will match your eyes, darling." And off she went to serve another giggling bride-to-be.

I looked at the cost of the dress after I tried it on and it fitted perfectly, but it was way too expensive for me to afford, even with the money my Dad had given me.

I approached the sales assistant and said, "I don't have enough money to buy this, but thank you for showing it to me, it was very kind of you." I turned to leave, but she grabbed my arm and said, "How much do you have on you?"

I looked into my purse and advised that I had a hundred dollars plus some loose change.

She smiled and said, "We have a sale on at the moment and everything is half price for you, dear." This woman had black hair and big blue eyes. Her nametag said Gloria. She smiled at me in a very motherly way.

I looked at her incredulously and so I left the store with a beautiful formal dress, and she even threw in a pair of matching shoes. I began to walk back towards the station.

A crowd had formed, people were lining the streets, and barriers were up. I crossed the road and walked past the throng and dodged and pushed past the press of people.

I hate crowds.

When I get to the Town Hall, I stop at the barrier to see what all the fuss is about and as I'm waiting I happen to notice a young police officer across from me. He is tall and strong looking with nice straight black hair, although it's cut short, but it's his eyes that stand out the most… they are a vivid blue like the sky. He smiles at me.

I smile back involuntarily and I feel a pull towards him. I start to walk towards him, but the parade for some sports club comes past and I get told to move back by Security as the crowd sways in time to a tribal beat. I decide to leave before I get squashed.

I stand on the platform waiting for my train to Jannali as I'd just missed one while I was on the escalator. I don't run on escalators or stairs. I'm clumsy. I wish I was going to my formal with that police officer. I sigh.

As I sit on the train near the window, a man sits next to me and I instinctively inch away, but then I feel something soft like skin touching my little finger and edge my hand towards my thigh.

I then feel his skin overlapping my hand. I panic and look at the young police officer and then at my hand. He's holding my hand in his. Why?

He leaned in towards me and said softly in to my left ear, "I've found you at last." I looked at him, stunned and unsure. I tried to jerk my hand away, but he held it firmly, then leaned into me again, and this time he said, "I've dreamt of you. I can't explain it… but every night, there you are." I realise he is being serious.

"You're serious. Why?" I asked timidly, "I've never ever met you before," but I begin to feel electricity from his proximity. It's pulling us together. I don't know why I know this, but I do.

He says, "I wish I knew why, but I feel, I feel like I've known you forever, like we are kindred spirits or something..." He rubs his thumb against my knuckles and this time I don't move away. It feels like heaven.

I am sitting next to this complete stranger, wondering 'What am I thinking?' I should take my hand away and get up and move to another seat, but… I can't. He has the most mesmerising eyes that seem to change depending on what he is thinking. I don't know how I know this, but it's true, it does seem like we know each other or that we've met each other previously.

He takes his hand away from mine and I instantly feel the electricity fade and I want to cry out to him to stay. I feel the need to tell him I need him. I want him to stay. Oh my, this is the first time I've held hands with a guy. He's beautiful… he's perfect.

He sighs and gets up and moves away from me. He turns back and I swear that we are the only people in the carriage even though I can hear chitchat all around us. He has a strange effect on me that I can't explain.

He walks up the stairs and the doors open as the train pulls into St Peters Station. He walks past my window and looks down at me and smiles.

Melancholy rips through me and I almost jump up and run after him, but the train closes its doors and I can't stand up. I watch him go up the stairs. He never stops looking at me, nor do I stop looking at him. I wish in hindsight that I'd given him my number.

I dream of him on the way home – Mr Perfect, caressing my hand and looking at me with those eyes, eyes filled with recognition and something else… home.

Will I ever see him again, my Mr Perfect? Will he take me away from all of this mundanity and give me what I yearn?

The ability to be me, carefree and loved for who I am… I've proven that I can't conform to what society expects of me.

That night I lie in bed and eventually fall asleep and dream of Mr Perfect. He is always in my dreams now. Sometimes I dream that he is lying next to me with his arms draped over my waist and I can feel his soft breath against my shoulder and his heart beating through my t-shirt and I want to feel his strong, protective arms around me and his throbbing (why is it always throbbing?), anyway, I want to feel his throbbing member against my thighs and know that he wants to make passionate love to me over and over again, and I wake up to feel the tightness deep down in my belly and the wetness between my legs.

Note to self – stop reading romance novels.

CHAPTER ONE

School Is Over

GRACE

"Rise and shine, Grace, it's time to get up now, it's the first day of the rest of your life!" yells my father from down in the kitchen. "If you're not up in five minutes I'll leave without you."

"Okay, Okay. I'm up, quit yelling," I mumble as I open my eyelids and face the sunshine coming in through my window. A bird is shrilly chirping on the branch in the yard and I wonder sarcastically if he is also telling me to "rise and shine".

I walk over to the bathroom door and knock loudly because my younger sister is in there doing her teeth. She mumbles, "In a minute," so I wait rather impatiently outside in the hallway and count to ten before I knock again and tell her that her time is up.

"Alright," she says and the handle clicks and I'm allowed in. Beth is wearing a red jumper over her school shirt and a pair of blue pants. She's in Year 10 now and it's an important year for her, just as it was for me last year. I've just completed my HSC but I didn't get enough to get into university and in the meantime I'm trying to find a job. Actually, in the meantime my parents want me to find a job. I just want to crawl back into bed and face all of this another day.

My parents were hoping for better things from me. When I got my results, there was great anticipation from them. I gingerly opened up the website and read my results. Their faces fell and warm platitudes ensued.

"It'll be okay, Grace, you can get in later or go to TAFE and get a degree that way," says my father with a false smile.

I went up to my room semi-relieved that my future wasn't going to turn out like my father wanted it to. He always expected me to be a lawyer like himself and we'd have our own practice, 'O'Malley's, Attorneys at Law.' I guess I'm just not that bright. I used to be bright. Heck, I was a bookworm and studied all the time. I just don't know where things went wrong. Maybe it was fate?

I remember just flopping onto the bed and I pretty much stayed there all throughout the New Year until today, and so my Dad offered to take me to the employment agency this morning – it's way too early – to show that I'm keen. He's all for making good impressions. I yawn as Beth walks past me and heads downstairs to breakfast.

I stand in front of the mirror and all I see is a failure. I get into the shower and wash my hair, a rich thick lather of soap is applied to my face and the water carries it down my neck and in rivulets around my breasts. The shower feels good.

The towel is damp. 'Damn Melody! She used my towel again, how many times do I have to tell her, my towel is the black one.' I step out and drip dry on the bathmat. I comb my hair free of tangles and begin to dry it with the hair dryer. 'Oh no! A pimple on my forehead!' My fringe barely covers it. I put foundation on in the hope it will stay hidden while I'm at the employment agency. I just hope I don't see anyone I know.

Choosing something to wear will be the hardest part of my morning routine. My closet is shared with my sister and most of her clothes are on the floor. Hmm, a black bra, a black pair of shoes, grey shirt, socks underwear, and finally my black skirt and jacket. I think when I get a job I'll move out.

I hate sharing everything with Beth. I'm neat and she's just downright disgusting.

I walk down the stairs and along the wall on my right are photographs of my family. My mother and father, grandparents, my annoying sister, and my older brother who moved out of home a couple of years ago and is partying hard at university while studying... yes, you guessed it... law.

Dad's in the kitchen seated at the table, eating his wholemeal toast with apricot jam and cracking open a boiled egg. His coffee smells good first thing in the morning.

Beth is talking to Mother about something which has her quite animated. It must be about boys. That's something I never had to worry about. My sister is popular. She didn't inherit the same genes as me, for starters her hair is blonde like our mother's and they still don't know where my auburn hair came from. Perhaps, with luck, I'll find out I'm adopted!

My father, George O'Malley, is almost a partner at the law firm he has worked at for nearly fifteen years and although now he has hardly any hair, he did have black hair like my brother, Eamon. I reach for a mug and pour the coffee into the cup, no sugar but a dash of milk, I sip and it tastes divine and I smile inwardly like the Cheshire cat.

My mother, Regina, walks towards me with a newspaper in her hand and my breakfast of eggs, bacon, and tomato. I take a slice of toast off the centre plate and spread apricot jam onto it. I peruse the newspaper. My mother has circled the 'Wanted' ads. There are a few jobs listed.

When breakfast was finished, my father kissed my mother on the lips and said goodbye after grabbing his briefcase and lunch. After all these years they still like each other.

My sister came next and got a kiss on her forehead which she ritually wiped off... so embarrassed. She's at that age.

My mother looks at me square in the eyes and smiles. "Hope you have a good day Grace, good luck and don't forget your lunch." I wonder what I've got today?

My father is waiting in the car and as I open the front passenger door my sister looks out at me and motions her head towards the back seat. I am anonymous again. That suits me fine, I guess. Pulling up in front of my old school gives me the shivers anyway. I just hope my sister enjoys her final years of school better than I did.

I was bullied by a select few and I'm hoping that's not a pattern for the rest of my life. I wonder what those girls are doing now. Part of me hopes that they end up getting their own medicine back in some dark alley, but that's not the way I've been brought up. Would I have to go to church at lunchtime to confess my evil thoughts about retribution? Would the big guy upstairs let this one slide? I rather hoped so.

My father looked in the rear-vision mirror and smiled as Beth slammed the door behind her and greeted a group of squealing girls in the carpark just before the bell chimed. She likes to be early at school as her groupies all hang out in the carpark and smoke and pick on the younger girls as they arrive. She also has to change into her sports gear because her first period today is PE.

We pull onto the road. My father starts a conversation. "Any job is a good job, Grace. It doesn't have to pay much, but you will be required to pay board when you do get a job, so keep that in mind. You'll want money to live too, not to mention a social life."

What's a social life, I wonder? I was never really the popular one in high school. I was a little weird. I never conformed. I was unique. 'Who's telling fibs now?' says my subconscious. Okay, I was socially awkward, clumsy, and tried too hard for others to like me. I was just unlucky in the popularity stakes. There's one like me in every high school in the country. I look out the window and we drive in a comfortable silence.

The traffic begins to get heavy as we near the station. Finding parking will be a matter of good fortune but eventually my father gets a spot... three blocks from the station. We walk in silence to the station platform and my father shows me where and how to buy a ticket and what to ask for. There are impatient sighs from behind us. It's Monday morning and I guess others are just as keen to get to work as my father is.

He's pretty sure they're going to make him a full partner this year and so he is putting in a little extra time and effort. The train rolls in alongside us. We take our seat downstairs and it fills up pretty quickly.

I scan the carriage and note that most of the passengers are men in suits, with their ipads and ipods playing what I think is music, although I can't be sure because all I can hear is thump, thump, then something different… no, it's another thump. It reminds me of the washing machine when it gets lopsided with towels and I chuckle to myself.

The train meanders through the outer suburbs of Sydney and my father is reading his business newspaper with interest. Commodities and takeovers fill his spare time. I think he secretly wanted to be a stockbroker, but his father was a lawyer before him.

He looks up as the train rolls into Town Hall Station and turns to me and smiles.

He gets up and so I blindly follow him up to the vestibule as the train lurches. The doors open at Martin Place Station and off we go up the escalators and outside the sun is shining and people are being swallowed into buildings all around us. He walks me to the employment agency and it's not open until 9am but he smiles and tells me to wait there until it opens and he'll see me tonight. It's now 8am.

So I wait and wait and open up my brown paper bag to see what my mother made me for lunch. It's a BLT on rye - oh well, it's not like I can afford to buy my own lunch anyway. So I sit on a bench and watch the world go by. Nervousness starts to creep in. What if I can't find a job? What if I'm no good at anything and I end up having to live off my parents for the rest of my life? Or, God forbid, sell myself up at the Cross? I saw a documentary about prostitution when I was at school and it made me think that, if I did become a lawyer, that was the area I wanted to work in - looking after the misfits or social pariahs whom no one else will defend.

But, I didn't get into university, so here I am sitting and swinging my legs and watching the world go by.

When the doors finally opened I walked inside, first client of the day, and I went to the noticeboard and looked. I then pulled a few cards off the board and at the front desk a middle-aged man asked me if I required assistance.

I asked him if I could see someone about these prospective jobs and I was given a form to fill out and a number. I was to sit and wait until someone could see me. I thought that was a bit rich, considering I was the only person in the office waiting. Anyway, I waited until my number was called. 'One' came up on the electronic screen and I got up and went to the far desk where another middled-aged man sat and smiled at me and I handed over the form and he typed the information into the database.

"What type of job are you interested in?" he asked.

"Gee, I'm unsure. I've just finished high school and I've not done much. I did work at Woolworth's once packing shelves and using the cash register. I've cleaned the local theatre as a part-time job after school too." His eyes suddenly lifted up and he smiled at me.

"Miss O'Malley, I think I've got the perfect job for you." He seemed so happy for me. I wonder if they're on commission or something?

"Uh, what is it?" I ask casually, trying to hide my excitement.

"It's a cleaning job with a large company right here in the city. They want someone to clean the office after 6pm each night and it involves vacuuming, emptying bins, cleaning the kitchen, restocking the photocopier paper, and whatever else is required. You'll just need to explain your past experience and show you're keen, they like that. Just turn up at that address at 5pm and ask for the janitor at the reception desk."

I nodded and took the card off him with the name and contact details on it.

CHAPTER TWO

Now What?

GRACE

'So what do I do now?' I say to myself as I leave the employment agency. I've stopped outside on the sidewalk, turning left and then right, wondering where I was to go. After all, I had the whole day to myself in the city, alone. I was to meet the outgoing janitor at 5pm. I could go visit my father, but he'd be busy in meetings. I decided after some deliberation to go window shopping in George Street… surely that would kill some time.

I walked several blocks and then turned into George Street itself. I found myself admiring the Apple store and the various aromas. I walked onward. I went into Myers and got a free makeover. The woman who did it was good. I came out looking like a model, or so she said. At least my pimple was hidden underneath foundation once again.

I remember going to the store at Miranda years ago with my mother and we got a makeover and when the woman had finished my mother looked at me and gasped in horror... I looked like a clown. I think it was the auburn hair, which was brighter than it is now. After all, most people in Miranda were blonde then, so those shop ladies could never quite choose colours to match me. This makeover though, by the lady from Myers, had used natural colours and a little pink and it really emphasised my cheekbones and eyes which were a dark green… sometimes.

After that I decided to go to the harbour and take in the view.

When I finally reached Circular Quay I had to sit down because the new shoes were beginning to rub and so I bought myself a drink and ate half a sandwich while I was serenaded by at least ten seagulls and thirty pigeons. The day was getting warm.

The city wasn't as packed as I'd expected it to be. I guess people were still on holidays. The schools, or at least the private schools, didn't go back for another week and I guess all those families were still sleeping in and taking it easy. I wish I could go back to bed and sleep. The world could wait just a few more days for me to catch up but no, my parents put their foot down last week when I spent an entire day in bed.

My mother was going from room to room picking up the washing and she came into my room with that thin lip of hers. The thin lip reveals itself when she's angry. I guess she waited until my father got home and had a 'quiet word' about my lethargy and how unhealthy it was, and that I had to look for a job or she'd kick me out or something.

My father cleared his throat at dinner, and so we all stopped eating and talking and looked at him expectantly. I was still in my pyjamas with my bedroom hair and I must have looked ridiculous, but his gaze zeroed in on me. I swallowed. My sister smiled because she knew it was me he wanted and she wasn't in trouble for anything.

"Grace, your mother and I feel it is time you got up off your bed and showered and did your hair and got out of the house. It's not healthy for you to sleep all day long and so, as of Monday, I'm going to take you to the city and you are going to get a job."

I just sat and inwardly cringed.

Now that I'm at Circular Quay I think to myself, 'Where should I go?' I look at my watch. It's nearly 10:30am. Too early for lunch; besides, I just ate half my sandwich. So, I decide not to go to The Rocks. I walk to the Opera House and I can smell the salt water and there are a lot of tourists waiting for ferries. Manly is very popular I note.

I continue to walk around Bennelong Point and admire the view just like every other tourist does. I offer to take a photograph for an Asian couple who have a little boy and then I move onward to the Botanical Gardens. I love the gardens, the trees and shade, the seats around the pond, and the cockatoos. Flying Foxes are clinging to the foliage and the array of colours on the flowers is amazing. Maybe I could go to TAFE or uni like my dad says and I could study plants!

My feet are really beginning to get sore, so I decide, as it is now 11.30am, that I will walk to The Rocks and find a shady spot underneath the Harbour Bridge and eat my lunch. I walk down Hunter Street.

I get to the corner of Hunter and George Streets and turn right. I walk back to the railway concourse at Circular Quay and, now almost limping from the blister forming at my heel. I go past pubs like the Fortune of War and restaurants. I can smell garlic and herbs and my mouth waters.

When I finally get to the Mercantile Hotel, I turn right again and head down the hill towards the pylons at the bottom of the Harbour Bridge. How majestic she looks. I sit on a wall looking out at the harbour and there is a refreshing sea breeze. I love the harbour and Sydney is just magnificent. I wouldn't want to live anywhere else. I fish out my sandwich and begin to eat my lunch.

Two police officers walk past. One looks over his shoulder at me. I pretend I don't notice. I hope he's looking at me as he looks rather cute from here!

A distant memory of a train and a police officer holding my hand pops into my brain fleetingly. Have I met that policeman before?

Anyway, people come and go and take photographs and play on the old cannons. The pylon has a huge metal door in front of it which opens to allow vehicular access, mostly painting vans. Other than that, people on foot were walking through a side gate with their identification tags allowing them access without having to sign in.

It's a very industrious area, what with the Sydney Buses driving past and the tourists and the ferries, cruise liners, yachts, and the palaces on water. Those floating palaces where the rich and famous spend their time cruising around islands and visiting exotic foreign ports, and I'm so jealous of that lifestyle. My mind wanders towards my interview this afternoon.

If I don't make a good impression with this old janitor this afternoon, I may not get a job for a very long time. How disappointed would my parents be? "Probably really pissed off at me, actually," I said to no one, but myself. My mother would mention "That my heart wasn't in it" and say, "They can tell that, you know!" My father would just shake his head.

After about an hour, I look at my watch and note it is only 1pm. I've got over three hours to go and so I decide to find a chemist and buy some band-aids for my blister. I hobbled back the way I came and found a chemist. I sat down on a chair and took my aching feet out of the black patent shoes and put band-aids all over them, practically. The shoes had rubbed my toes, my ankles, and my heels, and my feet look like they have measles with all the red splotches. Maybe I could become a pharmacist?

'What will I do now?' I ask myself.

I realised I had to use the bathroom, so I go to the closest pub and find myself squeezing against suits and apologising as they look down at me – some growl and some smile.

I look at myself in the mirror and run my fingers through my hair and place my hands inside my bra to push my breasts up. My deodorant goes on and instantly chills my underarms, and for that I'm grateful. Now, to get out of this pub alive and unmolested.

I stick my head up and place my arms in front of my chest kind of like a surgeon does after he's washed his hands and begin to say, "Excuse me," but I'm intercepted by a suit. His overhanging stomach is in front of my eyes like a protruding wall of white cotton and black jacket. I demurely look up towards his face and he's smiling down at me, a smile with a hidden agenda.

"You don't have to leave so soon, gorgeous, do you? Come have a drink with us?" I look at his friends in their identical suits. They all smile down at me and I feel claustrophobic and try to back up, but one of them is behind me and I swear blind he just felt my backside. "Don't touch me!" I turn around and glare at him.

On the street, two police officers stroll past and one of them stops and looks inside. The suit is blocking my path and keeps asking me to stay and each time I try to get around him he blocks me and asks me again to have a drink with him and his mates. He touches my hair and I say again, "Don't touch me!"

The police officer says, "If the young lady says no, she means no."

The suit turns his head and tells the officer, "I'm just being polite, Officer, she looks like she could do with a drink."

He turns back to his mates and they laugh.

I don't drink much. I'm eighteen and so I've only been out on one occasion, with my brother. There's not much in the way of night life where we live.

Plus, I didn't have any friends at school to hang out with. I mainly stayed home and listened to music or read books.

I politely but forcefully squeeze myself around him and begin to move forward. The wall of suits parts reluctantly and I get out onto the pavement.

The policeman asks if I'm okay and I nod and say thank you. I read his name tag - Senior Constable G. Dale. The other officer has his back to me and is answering a question – some tourist who is obviously lost. It looks like the same officer I saw when I was having my lunch. Taking a deep breath, I begin to walk back to St James and the building where I will meet the old janitor.

I turn around and he looks at me and smiles. Oh my... what a nice smile from this distance. I wonder what he'd look like up close and personal. My inner goddess swoons.

I begin to walk backwards. His face changes suddenly and it's like slow motion as his arm reaches out towards me.

I turn, also as if in slow motion also, just as a plank of wood sweeps about half an inch past my head. The man carrying it apologises and takes it into the building.

I feel my head. It has escaped injury. I turn back to him and see the relief on his face and I smile back at him. I shrug my shoulders and continue on my way as my heart begins jumping inside my chest with adrenalin... and something else. He looked really worried, like he cared about me, knew me. Oh my, he was a god!

My feet feel better but they are still rubbing. I decide to go into the Library and there I can get a book and sit and no one will mind. I still had a few hours to go and it was too hot and I was getting tired.

In the past few weeks since I finished my exams I've had a nanna nap after lunch every day except today. I didn't realise just how lazy I'd become.

I decided to go into the stacks and find a book and with some lengthy investigation I found something, and so I sat in a corner far away from the diligent researchers.

Sometime later a guy leaned towards me and asked me if the cubicle next to me was taken and I didn't look up from my book and just said, "No, go ahead." He chuckled to himself. He put his backpack on the desk and he unpacked his books and began to study. I thought to myself that he had a really nice voice, but, I was getting to a good bit in the book and so I ignored my curiosity.

After a while I looked at my watch, but it was only 3.45pm and so I relaxed a little and kept reading. A while later I looked at my watch again and it still said 4.45pm! I asked him if he had the time and this time I looked up at him. My jaw nearly unhinged itself from my face. He was twenty - something, with black hair cut in a short kind of way and built solidly but not in any way fat. He had the most beautiful blue eyes I'd ever seen and for some reason I couldn't talk or take my eyes off him. Had I seen him before?

Mr Perfect replied, "Ah, it's about 4.45pm, Miss." He called me 'Miss.' Wow, a man with manners, how perfect. I sigh but then he looks up at me with questions in his eyes, like why do I have to know the time, am I going to leave?

For a second I feel like throwing all my plans out the window to sit and stare at him.

"Oh shit!" I exclaim and all I hear are hundreds of "Shhhh." I said to Mr Perfect, "I've got an interview at 5pm at St James. I've got to go, thank you Mr Perfect."

I stopped dead. He looked up at me with an unreadable face, a face chiselled by the gods, just as I was realising what I'd said. I was mortified.

He smiled. I eventually found my legs and I made my way out to Macquarie Street, actually I ran out of the Library with desperation etched on my face and ran past the Parliament, Sydney Hospital, and the Mint and then cut through Hyde Park to come out at the lights at the corner of Elizabeth and Park Streets, and I crossed at the lights.

I ran across the road and stopped, reached into my pocket for the job card, and it wasn't there. I looked around everywhere, retraced my steps, and then I bumped into this solid wall of man.

'Ouch!" I proclaimed whilst rubbing my nose, ready to abuse this man for not looking where he was going. Looking up with a scowl, I realised with horror that it was Mr Perfect.

"Hello again," I said shyly and swallowed, my face going a darker shade of red.

"I think this belongs to you, Miss, you dropped it in the Library," said Mr Perfect and he smiled at me and my face turned scarlet. "Oh and, by the way, my name's Andrew, not Mr Perfect, but if you'd rather call me that, that's okay too." He walked back towards Hyde Park, shaking his head and laughing.

I found myself mesmerised by his long legs and taut buttocks as he crossed the road. Almost wishing that Mr Per... Andrew... would turn around and smile at me. To my surprise, shock, and horror he did and he looked like he was going to come back, but then he turned and he smiled that smile and shook his head again laughing and kept walking the way he'd come.

I felt like an absolute idiot. I was sure I was going to drop dead on the spot from embarrassment.

I took a deep breath noting that my nipples had hardened and were poking through my blouse. Great. Perky personality and perky breasts, that's sure to get me the job!

I looked down at the card, noting that the interview was just around the corner. I hurried, with only minutes left before I would be late. My father always told me, "Never be late."

So, I went inside the building and cleared my throat at the receptionist. She looked up and smiled and asked me how she could assist me. I asked her for Mr Bennett the janitor and she dialled a number and told me to wait in the vestibule.

A few moments clicked by and the lift bell goes 'ding' and suits get out and leave the building. The next lift went 'ding' and I stretched my neck to see if it was the janitor, but it was just more suits.

After what seemed like a week, the far lift made a distant 'ding' and out of the goods lift an elderly man with white hair and a grey uniform came towards me. He looked left and right and then I stood up and he saw me. I walked towards him and presented my hand for him to shake.

He stood, looked me over, and grunted a hello.

"You've cleaned before?" he asked.

I replied, "Yes, for the local cinema near where I live, sir." I didn't actually work in the cinema or clean for them, but I did go there a lot to see movies and I did wipe things and cleaned up the seats… so what if I embellished a little on my application. My father had said it was okay to do that and he was a lawyer, so he had to be right.

"You don't mind being in a building late at night all by yourself?" he grunted.

"No, I actually like to be by myself, sir."

"I'll give you one month's trial – come with me."

So, we got back into the goods lift and he took me up to the executive floor, Level 10. The lift bell dings as the doors open and he shuffles into the vestibule.

"On each floor you've got a door marked 'Cleaner.' Here is your key. Don't lose it."

He walks to the door and opens it and inside is a bucket, cleaning cloths, toilet paper, mops, brooms, bin liners, and chemicals.

"You start each evening walking around the floor and emptying all the bins and the shredder. Then you put photocopy paper in the machines and cupboards. Vacuum where you see fit. Then you replace the paper cups at all the water stations, but don't lift the water vats, that's too heavy for a slight thing like you. If your bin here (and he points to the trolley) is full, take it down to the basement and put it into one of the larger bins marked 'Recycled Paper.'"

"Next you wash the foyer floors and vestibules, kitchens and toilets. Clean the kitchens and toilets, both male and female, and the sinks. Don't touch their desks, we do too bloody much for them as it is," he grumbled. "Vacuum the utility room as well."

I nodded diligently.

He said, "You'll start at 6pm and it shouldn't take you that long to clean all ten floors and the foyer down stairs," and then as an afterthought, "You can get home late at night, can't you?"

I nodded. I'd just get a train and my parents would pick me up. That is, until I got my own place, which was high on my agenda.

He seemed satisfied and so we walked through the offices and he showed me where the toilets were and the kitchens, and by the time he had finished it was 6 pm.

He said, "I've got to start cleaning soon, so come back tomorrow and we'll put you through your paces. Bring your own dinner with you as you'll get a break at Level 5."

I asked him "What time do you usually finish, sir?" He looked at me and said, "Midnight, sometimes later, sometimes earlier." I nodded and then we turned back to the lift and went down to the basement.

He showed me his storeroom where he keeps the supplies. He restocks the smaller rooms each week so that he doesn't have to keep coming down to the basement, which takes too much time. I could see the sense in that.

Mr Bennett said, "If you are about to run out of something, talk to the Acquisitions Officer on Level 7. His name is Mr Brady, but, you have to be here at least by 4pm to present him with your list as he finishes at 5pm on the dot." I nod again.

He says goodbye in the foyer and tells me that he'll contact the agency and advise them that he'll put me on for a trial and I leave, with the sun about to hide behind the buildings as it neared sunset and catch the train home.

My mother collects me from the station and asks me a million questions and is so excited that I got a job and can't wait to tell my father.

As we drive into the garage, the light goes on automatically and she jumps out with a flourish and goes straight into the kitchen to tell Father that I'd got a job.

When I sit at the table, my dinner is placed in front of me. Steak, mashed potato, veg, and I'm famished and scoff the lot as I tell them both about the building and the janitor and that I start on trial tomorrow at 6pm sharp.

I'm tired after dinner, so I go upstairs. I decide to have a shower and my clothes fall to the floor in a heap. The water is hot and steam rises and the glass fogs over. I've got a smile on my face and am feeling quite proud of myself.

My bed feels fresh because my mother washed my sheets, and as I relax into the pillow I begin to remember the man in the Library – Mr Perfect or Andrew. I fish the card out of my bag that he had touched and reread it again.

There was a number on the reverse side of the card which hadn't been there when I left the employment agency. Could it be Andrew's mobile number? Why? I only just met him. My subconscious says to me, 'You are an attractive young woman, that's why.'

I get up and look at myself in the mirror. I turn left and then right and fluff my hair out again and stand up straight and my breasts pop out all perky again and I feel self-conscious, I blush. But I won't call him.

My subconscious says, 'Phone him; what have you got to lose?'

I'm a little shy around guys. I've never kissed one and never been on a date and I'm pure.

Part of me wants to experience all those things, but I'm kind of scared. And I always imagined it'd be special, under the stars on a four-post bed with silky sheets and champagne, and Mr Perfect and I just staring at each other. Mr Perfect hasn't had a face for a long time but now, after meeting Andrew... his face has taken shape.

I lie down in bed and within moments I'm asleep.

ANDREW

"Sergeant, I'm…" I begin to introduce myself, but the Captain says, "Senior Constable Andrew Jennings?" I nod. "Welcome to The Rocks. I'll show you around the station, follow me."

The station isn't that big and before long I've stowed away my civilian clothes and strapped my utility belt on and ensured my gun is loaded and in place in the holster with the safety on. My shoes are shined and my uniform is pressed, thanks to my mother. At twenty-three years of age you'd think I'd have moved out, but it's just the two of us. I'm the man of the house since my Dad passed away five years ago from cancer.

I've been a Constable for two years and I've finished my stint in a country Local Area Command and now been transferred to The Rocks. I only just moved back in with her a few weeks ago after I got my transfer, so it's going to take me a while to get used to the noises and smells of the big city. We originally lived in the small Southern Highlands town of Raven but my mother and father decided to move to the big smoke when I was a baby. My father had gotten a job up here, so they bought a place in St Peters.

I've got two cousins who live in the southern suburbs, but we aren't that close… due to our busy lives I guess. One of them is an ambo and from time to time we cross paths and the other one is still at university studying something – I think Mum said it was journalism.

I wanted to have the opportunity to work in a different kind of busy station.

I'll stay here at this station for a while and once I take my exams for promotion l might be transferred to Head Office or one of the specialty areas like Forensics or Homicide, or just stay here. I have options.

I meet up with Senior Constable Gerry Dale and we go to our briefing. It's always busy in the city. We seem to have a lot of bored teenagers committing crimes like graffiti, assault, petty thievery, to name a few. It seems that that's the message our Captain is imparting this morning and I'm so excited and eager to be on my feet.

We leave the station and walk towards the Harbour Bridge. I admire the view. It's 7.30am and the city is just starting to wake up. I love mornings and the dew on the grass shimmers like diamonds and the city is remarkably quiet for a moment. I stop and take a deep breath and Gerry chuckles and says, "Mate, once you've been here for as long as I have, you won't even smell it and then you know you've been here way too long." I disagree with him and feel that I'd never get sick of this view… of this place called Sydney.

Gerry and I stop to talk to another pair of officers. Some of the beats overlap and I'm introduced to them and they welcome me to the city. It's coffee time and Gerry and I go get something to eat and all is quiet.

We get asked a lot of questions by tourists and help them with their maps and advice about buses and where they can find a good place to eat. I look to Gerry for that information as it's my first day here. We head back to the station a few times during the morning and then we are off again, walking the beat. Yet another ship is at the overseas terminal and the main street becomes busy.

Gerry watches the passengers and the vehicles, making sure they're all safe and gives advice on where the nearest railway station is. We walk towards the foreshore. Before I know it, it's time to head back to the station to do paperwork and have another coffee.

Walking back, I notice a young woman sitting on the wall looking out to the harbour with the most unusual colour hair. As we get closer, I see that it is auburn and somewhere in my psyche I nod my approval. I like that colour hair. She's beautiful. Have I met her before? We walk onward. I don't know why, but I just have to look back at her. Gerry notices and asks me if something is wrong. I just say casually, "Nope, just looking at the scenery." We walk on in silence. My heart is fluttering. That's never happened before… except once on a busy train.

After we've finished our paperwork and had a coffee, we set out for another patrol and Gerry stops outside a pub and is looking at something. I get asked by some tourists about how to get to the Art Gallery and the Museum and so I'm giving them directions and showing them on the map. I've got my back turned away from the front door and Gerry is talking to a pub patron. I look up for just a second and down the footpath looking at me is that girl again, the one with the auburn hair. I think she's checking me out. My chest swells and I smile.

I come back to earth as she begins to walk backwards, still staring at me, and my heart jumps when I realise a man carrying a plank of wood is about to whack her head and she recognises my gesture and turns and it misses her by millimetres and she blushes and walks further away and I ask Gerry what was wrong and he replied, "Some guy in there wouldn't let a young woman get by and he just needed a little nudge." Gerry smiled.

Well, my first shift ends and I get changed into my jeans and shirt. I lock my ammo in my locker and hand my gun into the armoury.

Gerry enquires what train I'm going to get and I tell him I'm going to the Library to do some studying and we say goodbye and I walk past the pubs, past the chemist, and head towards Circular Quay. I turn left at the Quay and head towards Macquarie Street and the Botanical Gardens.

The Library isn't too far to walk to.

I get to the Library and decide to be a little tourist myself and so I walk into the Mitchell Library. The ceiling is huge and the shelves of books… I'm in awe. I love reading. I could stay here forever, but… duty calls. I walk towards the main Library and it looks like everyone in Sydney has decided to get out of the heat and it's not what I had imagined. I walk about looking for an empty desk and as it happens there is one next to a girl… who looks familiar, but the lights are dim near the stacks.

I lean down and ask if I might take this desk beside her, and she responds without looking up at me, which makes me laugh. City people. I shake my head. She must be really, really engrossed in that book.

I sit down and get my books out of my backpack. I begin to study.

I'm grateful that the young woman is quiet and I get really involved in my own studies until she asks me a question, "Do you have the time?" Her voice sounds soft and sensual and the hairs on the back of my neck prickle. I looked at my wristwatch and it was 4.45pm. I look up and she's staring at me and I stare at her. Her eyes are a beautiful green, like a tree frog or a fresh spring leaf, but poetry isn't my strong point.

I smile and she blushes. Then, as if I'd said something completely incoherent, she looks at me and her eyes go wide.

I'm thinking something is wrong. She stands up, shoving her stuff into her bag and says, *"Oh shit! "*

Lots of people say, "Shhhhh" as she begins to panic. I want to ask her what is wrong, but then she says something I'm not expecting, *"I've got an interview at 5pm at St James. I've got to go, thank you Mr Perfect."*

She stopped dead. I could see her face. Those red cheeks turning ashen white with horror and I can't help but smile and laugh at that. She thinks I'm perfect! She's not so bad herself. She runs out of the Library and in her haste she drops a square card.

It is her contact and address for her job interview. I feel responsible for her dropping it because she was all flustered for some reason. I think I'd like to see her again. There's something about her that makes my heart skip a beat and so I jot down my mobile number. I'll tell her it's in case she's ever in trouble but, between you and me, it's because I want to see her again. I'd like to run my fingers through that auburn hair. The book she left on the desk is a classic. I'm impressed. I take note of the building managers named on the card, Halstead Holdings. I don't know why, but it's part of my job to be observant.

I decide to follow her and hand the card over. She might need it. I bet she hasn't memorised the address and other important details.

I walk out of the Library and down Macquarie Street. Eventually I spot her walking through Hyde Park and so I follow as she crosses Elizabeth Street. When she gets to the other side of the road, she realises she hasn't got her card. I cross after her and I watch her, mesmerised.

She follows her steps backwards. She comes up to my chest and smacks right into me. I think she hurt her nose. The face she gives me makes me smile and then I hand over the card.

She looks shy all of a sudden and says, "Hello again."

"I think this belongs to you, Miss, you dropped it in the Library," I said and smiled at her. "Oh and by the way, my name's Andrew, not Mr Perfect, but if you'd rather call me that, that's okay too." I walk back towards the Library.

I can feel she is still looking at me and so I turn around and her face is scarlet and I shake my head and laugh. I hope she phones me… damn, I forgot to mention she could phone me if ever she's in trouble. I turn around to go back but change my mind.

I don't know what it is about her. She looks like the girl I saw at the Harbour Bridge and near the pub and it all clicks into place. I never forget a … hmmm… I muse and think to myself... it was that auburn hair.

CHAPTER THREE

My First Night

GRACE

My first night on my own and here I am standing outside the building, again. I open the door, smile at the receptionist, and press the button for the goods-lift to take me down to the basement.

I walk inside the lift and the doors slowly close. There is no elevator music and quite frankly it needs a woman's touch. No glass, no air, no carpet, and definitely lots of dust. I'm going to have to clean this as well if I'm going to work here for the rest of my life; this lift will have to be cleaned.

When the doors open again, I am in the semi-dark basement. I turn on the lights and walk towards the room marked 'Cleaner' and inside the room amongst the stores is a locker. I find my overalls and so I change into them and wheel the trolley laden with rags, mops, and other assorted accessories for cleaning the building. I take the lift to the tenth floor and begin going from desk to desk and emptying the bins. I clean the kitchen, wash the floor, move on to the toilets and replace the toilet paper, move on to the utility room and restack the photocopiers and vacuum the floor, restack the cupboard, supply more paper cups, and… sigh... one floor done, nine to go.

I move down to the next floor and repeat the process. I could get used to this very quickly. Mr Bennett the janitor said he would be checking up on me to ensure I carried out his instructions while I'm on trial.

When I got to the fifth floor I found a chair in the time-out room and ate my sandwiches and had a cuppa and put my feet up.

Only four more floors to go and then the reception area. It was 9 o'clock. I could finish these lower floors by 11, easy, and be on my way home. I could do this. I smiled to myself and got thinking about Andrew, aka Mr Perfect, and fished the card out of my pocket again and almost reached for my mobile.

Do girls call guys these days? I always imagined the guy would do the chasing. I start thinking about the book I finished last week. It was filled with gallant knights and brazen ladies and romance, so much romance it made my heart flutter.

I got up and cleaned the rest of the floors and the reception area. I also cleaned the glass to ensure it was sparkling and the receptionist had a better view of the outside.

When I had finished, I went back down to the basement and as I rode in the lift I cleaned its floor and wiped the dust off the controls and handrail. A little bit each night and I would have it sparkling. I got changed out of my overalls and washed my hands to get rid of the bleach smell. I caught the lift up again and pressed the button at the main doors leading out to the street. It was 11 o'clock on the dot.

I walked to Martin Place Station. I sat near the Guard's compartment and was very aware and alert the whole way home. I phoned my Dad and he met me at the station. He said sleepily to me, "We'll see what we can do about getting you a car so that you can drive to work. I don't think this is going to work long-term."

I yawned.

I dreamt of Mr Perfect again as I fell into a heavy sleep.

My head against his chest in Macquarie Street. He puts his strong arms around me and kisses me passionately. He looks down at me and gives me that smile. I'm smitten.

The next thing I know it's 2am. I wonder what he's doing now? He's probably fast asleep. Yawn. I roll over and start dreaming of him riding a white stallion and whisking me away towards our castle to make passionate love to me over and over again.

The next night I pulled the cleaning cart out of the lift on the seventh floor, Marketing and Accounts. I started to empty the bins and as I got to the kitchen I heard strange noises. I crept up to the door and leaned my head in just behind the fern, so that whoever or whatever was in there wouldn't see me.

My eyes opened and my jaw dropped. In the kitchen there was a woman with her blouse opened and her skirt hitched up past her hips and a man in a suit was leaning against her with his trousers around his ankles, his bare bottom visible and his cheeks clenching in and out, and they were having sex! He was holding her arms up with one huge hand and she seemed, I don't know, not really enjoying it. She was crying. He was saying things to her like, "You wanted this, parading yourself around my desk each day. Now you've got me," as he slammed inside her.

He was moaning and groaning. She was whimpering. He backhanded her with his other hand and then he grunted and moved out of her and let her fall to the floor and bent down to her and said, "Next time don't wear that fucking perfume near me, DO. YOU. HEAR. ME?" The woman nodded and he yelled again, "I. DIDN'T. HEAR. YOU." The woman spoke up louder, saying she wouldn't wear it again.

He kicked her in the ribs. I was just turning around to go and get help when the man said, "So, you like to watch, bitch, you like what you're seeing, you want some of me too, huh?" 'Oh shit, he saw me,' I said to myself and swallowed.

I walked away as quickly as I could, but the man came to the kitchen door and towards me, zipping up his fly. I pressed the button for the lift, willing it to come and whisk me away from this. As the lift opened, he put his arm across the door obstructing my entry. I looked down at my feet, terror filled me, and I started to shiver.

He said, "Hey, you haven't been here that long, don't tell anyone about this," as he pointed his thumb in the direction of the kitchen, "She asked for it. She likes it rough. Anyway, if you tell, they won't believe you, you know why?"

I shook my head.

"'Cause I'm the boss here and I'm a great guy. No one will ever believe you and maybe if you're good I'll give you some." He grips his shaft through his pants and squeezes it to emphasise just what he means. "If you tell anyone, I'll get you fired, you got me? Then I'll come after you. I'll be waiting outside for you one night. If you're a good girl it might even be tonight, yeah I think it will be, and I'll fucking have you too. You deserve everything you get for being a nosy parker." I could feel his breath on my cheek and I nodded. He had alcohol on his breath. He slapped his hand off the back of my head. I teetered for a moment and nearly fell face first into the lift.

He took his arm off the door and pushed me back, and I fell against my trolley and knocked it over while he took the lift. I didn't move until he was down a floor. I went to the kitchen to check on the woman and she was crying and trying to cover herself. I helped her up and she gripped her ribs.

43

I didn't know what to do. I took her to the foyer and phoned her a taxi. That's all she wanted and begged me to not tell anyone or he'd hurt her and probably me as well. I rubbed the back of my head because it still smarted.

I left once the taxi turned up, went upstairs and got off on Level 7 to retrieve my trolley, and then I went to Level 6 and my heart was thumping inside my chest.

That night I finished a little later and I knew I'd missed my train as the clock ticked past 11.45pm. I was tired. I was flustered and began to panic and cry. My parents would be worried. I was too scared to leave the building. What if he was waiting outside for me like he said he would?

I don't know why I did it, but I fished out the card and I dialled the number and he answered the phone.

"Hello," I said tentatively.

"Hello, who's speaking?" said a male voice.

"I... I..." Fear grips me and I hang up on him, my Mr Perfect. What was I thinking? It's nearly midnight and here I am phoning a complete stranger to ask him to... to what? To help me. I'm crying again and shivering.

My phone rang and it scared the hell out of me. I answered it timidly.

"Hello?"

It's him again.

"Why'd you hang up on me? What's wrong?"

I start to cry over the phone and I ask him to help me.

"Of course, where are you? Are you outside the building where you went for the interview?"

"No, I'm in the foyer," I reply.

His voice changes slightly... I don't know, more business-like.

"I'll be there soon. Stay where you are."

I thanked him and he hung up. I stood inside the doors. The only way out is to push a button. I'm cold and I begin to shiver even though I've got a jacket on. I'm tired. I should have walked away and not got involved. If I hadn't gone back to Level 7 after he left, I would have made my train. But I was still on trial and I had to finish it.

Mr Perfect will be angry with me and what was I thinking? I don't know this guy from a bar of soap. What if he's a murderer? Or, after I tell him what happened, he'll say, "It's all your fault, you shouldn't have spied on them," I said out loud, a bad impression of his voice. He won't believe me. I'll have to call my parents to come and get me and they won't be happy with me, or they'll over-react. I cried. "Or maybe I could stay here on a couch until morning?" I said out loud to no one.

What if the man comes back? He has a pass to get into the building. I started to panic all over again.

Approximately twenty minutes later a man approached the building and shone his torch in my direction. He looks familiar but in the dark it's hard to tell and then, as he gets closer to me, he smiles and I know who he is. I'm relieved and I open the doors.

I take one step, just one step towards him, and my legs turn to jelly and all the adrenalin rushing through my veins has left me feeling spent.

I start to sink to my knees towards the pavement and he catches me just before I meet the cold hard concrete.

"I'm so sorry for disturbing you. I… I'm in trouble, aren't I?"

"Trouble?" he asks, "Why would you think that?" He stands me up gently, not taking his arms off me.

"Because you were asleep." He takes me in his arms in a warm embrace. I begin to shiver and cry a little. "Hey, I'm here now, so tell me what's wrong. What happened?" He looks into my eyes with concern.

"I went to clean the kitchen on Level 7 and this man and a woman were having sex, but I think he forced her, I saw him hit her and kick her in the ribs and she just laid there on the floor and I walked away to get some help but he saw me and he wouldn't let me into the lift and he said that if I told anyone he'd get me fired. I'm worried that he will do what he said and I don't feel safe working at night now and I've missed my train." I start to cry again. "He slapped the back of my head and pushed me to the floor and I fell onto my trolley."

"It's all right, anyone would be afraid after seeing that and he had no right to threaten you like that or hurt you." He put his hand at the back of my head and gently rubbed it. "I gave you my mobile number in case you were ever in trouble, and you can call me at any time, day or night, okay. I'm a police officer. What's your name?"

"Grace," I replied. I sniffed again and then a fresh wave of tears came out and he held me closer.

"He said that if I was…"

"'What?" and he looks me in the eyes again.

"'If I was good he'd give me some and he grabbed himself... down there and then he said I'll come after you just because I can.'"

I really started to shiver and shake now. "He also said, 'I'll be waiting outside for you one night, might even be tonight, and I'll fucking have you.'"

Andrew held me once again in his warm embrace, hushing me, and then he kissed my head. I could have stayed in his arms all night. I felt safe. He said something about my parents but I just didn't move.

"The woman you mentioned, do you think if I spoke to her tomorrow she'd make a complaint against him?" asked Mr Perfect. I shook my head and said, "She said that I should keep quiet and to not tell anyone or he'd hurt her and me."

Andrew looked at his watch.

"Let's get you home. Phone your parents and let them know you are okay and you'll be home soon."

I did as he asked.

I get bundled into his car and he drives me home. As we pull into my driveway, my parents are out the front waiting. They have questions on their faces, expecting the worst.

I get out of the car and run up to them and hug them and tell them I'm fine.

Andrew approaches my parents and pulls out his police badge and explains that I telephoned the station (he doesn't tell them that I had his private mobile number) and advised them that I'd had a little bit of a fright at work.

He said that he will look into the situation and that I was not in trouble and everything would be okay. My parents were grateful.

I thanked him. Andrew looked at me, really looked at me, like he was committing my face to memory or that he wanted something, but my parents were leading me inside. I felt just awful and wanted to say a thousand things to him but I just couldn't.

I told my parents everything that happened and they were understandably in shock and I went up to bed. I texted Andrew - *Thank you. I won't disturb you again.* I got a text back - *It wasn't a bother. If you ever need help don't hesitate to call... I mean it.*

I laid on my bed. There he was leaning against the kitchen sink slamming himself against that woman. He was moaning and groaning and in a blur it was me in her place screaming and crying out for him to stop and I was hitting him and trying to push him away but to no avail. I could see his sneer and smell his stale breath and after he'd satisfied himself he left me to put my clothes on and cry on the floor.

I tossed and turned all night.

When I finally woke up, I had a text from Andrew asking if I had slept okay. I smiled and texted him back - *No, not really, I had nightmares and today I think I might take up self-defence classes ha ha.*

Andrew replied - *Not a bad idea. I'll get you some literature or maybe I could teach you some moves ha ha. Meet me out the front of your office this afternoon. Take care and I'll talk to you later.*

I told him I started at 5.30pm.

I felt my heart skip a beat.

Wow, Mr Perfect is asking me to "'take care'" like he's worried about me or something and saying he'd teach me some moves. Why is it that he can make those words sound so exciting and erotic? He's going to see me this afternoon to give me some literature. That voice inside my head says, 'Nah, he's probably like that with everyone. He's a police officer, it's his job to serve and protect.'

I decided that I wasn't going to quit the job. I wasn't going to give 'him' the satisfaction of thinking that he'd frightened me. I got the train as usual and walked towards the front of the building and there was Andrew leaning against a pillar. He smiled that smile. I swallowed. I stared at him and he leaned down and spoke to me softly in my ear and said, "Grace. Breathe," and he placed his finger on my jaw and traced it down to my chin and I just wanted to melt. I smiled back at him and thanked him again for coming to get me and for being there and everything. He seemed touched and nodded.

He reached into his bag and handed me the pamphlets before he left. He turned away and said he was going to the Library. I turned and went through the front door and went down to the basement to change and get my trolley and supplies.

I had an uneventful night, thank God. I was a little nervous about leaving the building but I couldn't stay inside all night; besides, there were late-night shoppers around.

Andrew texted me and I was happy to report that all was quiet and I got myself home and then texted him that I was safe. He wrote back - *Happy to hear it, now get some sleep.*

He seems so bossy!

After a few weeks I was firmly into my routine, getting my work done earlier, and now even the goods lift was pretty to get into.

A woman's touch was all that was needed. I cleaned the other lifts too.

Andrew and I sometimes met up before work and talked when he was finished his shift. We were becoming friends although I wanted more. He was a gentleman and never tried to kiss me or touch me except when he'd hold my hand or when he touched my arm or face, my neck… or my heart.

He sometimes met me at the front doors and took me home too. He was so gallant and charming and old-school. I think I was beginning to like him. No, who was I kidding? I did like him, a lot.

We talked for ages and one night as he dropped me off at home I laughed and he seemed to be miles away and then he twined his fingers in my hair, saying, "I love your auburn hair." I went another shade of red and he asked me if we could go on a date one night and have dinner and talk. I replied, "Yes," then said, "Goodnight," and ran inside. He texted me each night to wish me a good sleep, as did I to him.

In a text message the next day he advised that he had passed his exams and had gotten a promotion. He was now responsible for other officers and had more responsibility. He told me that his real dream was to work in Homicide.

When he met me outside work, I told him I thought that working in Homicide would be scary, what with seeing dead bodies and stuff. He just smiled and put his hand in mine as he walked me to my door.

ANDREW

I was in bed fast asleep and at first I didn't register, but then my mobile phone goes off. I react before my brain has time to wake up fully. It's a girl, could it be that girl?

Something is wrong. She hangs up on me.

I phone her back puzzled. She starts crying. Now I'm really worried.

I move off my bed and pace my room. I feel all protective and I can't explain why and so I tell her I'll be there in a few minutes.

I throw on jeans, a t-shirt, shoes, and grab my keys. I go downstairs. My mother turns her bedroom light on and asks me what's wrong.

I tell her it's just work.

She mumbles something and goes back to sleep.

I park at St James Station and walk towards the building where a young woman is standing behind glass doors. It is her, the girl with the auburn hair, and she looks so scared and cold. She's shaking like a leaf. "What could have happened to make her so scared? I say out loud.

I approach her with caution so that she knows I'm not going to hurt her.

She looks terrified but then relief spreads across her face. She opens up the doors. Is it relief that someone has come to help her or relief that it's me? I'd like to think it's because it's me.

Just as she steps out of the protection of the foyer and onto the pavement, her knees give out on her and she just slides down, but I grab her before she ends up on the concrete and hold her and then when I think she's okay I stand her up, never taking my arms off her.

She's sorry for disturbing me. My heart aches as I hold her to me. She tells me what happened and I tell her that she did the right thing and that he had no right to do what he did to that woman or her. I comfort her and tell her she should phone her parents and that I would drive her home.

She's not really coherent so I step into police mode and tell her what to do and she responds and before I know it we are sitting in my car. She holds my hand the whole way home and I stroke my thumb over her knuckles and tell her everything will be okay and I'll do whatever I can. I tell her again that she did the right thing and that if ever she needs me all she has to do is text or phone and I'll be there for her, day or night.

She nods and tears form again. I pull over and get out of the car. I open up her passenger door, wipe her tears with my thumbs, and just hold her again to comfort her. I want to kiss her tears away but refrain. I never want to let her go. I've only just met her, but a part of me knows I've been searching for her forever. I feel relief that I have her now, but I have to get her home. When she had composed herself again, I drove off.

I'd never been in Jannali before. Her parents' house looks nice from what I can see.

We drive into the driveway and I get out and open her door. She gets out and runs to her parents and hugs them. I go up to talk to them and assure them that everything is okay, she's not in trouble, she's just shaken up, and that I'll look into it and they are appreciative. They seem nice.

I look at her, wanting to hold her again, but she's bundled off inside and so I walk to my car and drive back home.

I park out the front of my house and stroll in. I put my keys down and get back into my sweat pants and climb into bed, but I can't sleep. I receive a text from her and then I send one to her in reply.

I smile and reinforce to her that everything is okay and that if she needs me to just call. I've made arrangements to see her before her work and give her some literature about self-defence. I can't wait. I really want to get to know her. As I drift off to sleep, I decide there and then that, if I can, I'll be at her work each night to ensure she is safe, either drive her home myself or see her to her train.

CHAPTER FOUR

Our First Date

GRACE

I was going to meet up with Andrew as it was Friday night and he wanted me to go out with him, like it was our first proper date and he wanted to talk to me. I was curious about what. I imagined all different scenarios and of course they were awfully romantic. I was so excited. We had planned to go to a late dinner at The Rocks and I was so looking forward to a big plate of bolognese with parmesan cheese and herb bread and copious amounts of ice cream. Andrew had laughed at me when I told him that was what I wanted to do on our first official date. He has a beautiful laugh.

I got a text at lunchtime from him, telling me how much he was looking forward to seeing me. I smiled from ear to ear the whole evening.

I had started work at 4pm instead of my normal time and would therefore be finished at 9pm. I was excited about the fact that he was going to pick me up and walk with me hand in hand. We might even kiss. God, I hoped so!

I finished all the floors and that guy from Level 7 was nowhere to be seen as I cleaned the floor and I bypassed his office because the thought of him gave me the shivers. I went down in the lift to the basement after I'd finished all the floors. I changed out of my overalls and while I'm getting more supplies to restock the floors ready for Monday I hear the lift go 'ding'.

That was strange, no one ever came down here.

I stuck my head out and said, "Hello, is someone there?" There was no answer. I turned back to getting the toilet paper and other supplies and the lights in the storeroom went off.

Oh great, I thought, just my luck.

I turned to get a torch off the bench, but as I got to the door someone grabbed me. The only lights working were the emergency lights and I could tell it was him, him from Level 7.

I yelled, "What are you doing? Let me go! Take your hands off me." I struggled to get loose and he gripped my wrists tighter so that struggling was fruitless. "You're hurting me!"

"Good," he said.

"What do you want? I didn't tell anyone, leave me alone, please, leave me alone. I didn't tell anyone." He let my hands go and wrapped his arms around my waist so that I was flush up against his body. I went to my pocket, but realised that I had left my mobile in the bag which was still in my open locker, and then he savagely took my hands in his again and was now holding onto both wrists and I couldn't get to it. I kicked out, hoping to hurt him.

He grabs me around my waist again with his free hand and lifts me off the ground. He kisses me harshly on my lips. He says, "I've seen you parading yourself past all the men in the office as you empty the bins, you prick-teaser. You wanted me to follow you all the way down here, you fucking tart." I keep my mouth shut. I turn my head left and right, struggling to escape. He pushes me against the wall and knocks the wind out of me and holds me in place. He tries to kiss me again.

My mobile phone tells me there is a text message. I try to stretch my arm to reach it, but to no avail.

He has his forearm across my neck and is holding me firmly. My hands are now free but he has me pinned so that I can barely breathe. If I should lose consciousness, he will have me – no matter what. I try to pull him off me. But he is just too strong. It's nearly 9pm. I had rushed through my work so that I could get out earlier. I hope that Andrew is not cancelling our date due to work – I dearly hope he turns up shortly and realises that something is wrong and waits for me and doesn't think I've left without him! I think I'm going to need a friend tonight.

He chuckles and starts to fondle my breasts with his free hand. He pulls my blouse open in one huge tug and the buttons pop off onto the floor. His hand is fondling my left breast and then my right. My nipple responds against my will and he smiles. I just know he's smiling. I can feel his erection against me and he tells me that I want him. I cry out that I don't.

He leans his face down towards my breasts and suckles my left nipple, pulling it, biting it, and it hurts through the fabric. My mobile rings. His chin is scratchy like sandpaper. His breath reminds me of dead fish after a week in the sun.

I start to cry. I am resigned to my fate. My mobile rings again.

He fumbles at the back of my bra and ends up ripping it over my breasts in his haste. It hurts. My lungs are crying out for air. He takes my breasts and squeezes them painfully between thumb and finger, sucking like the pig that he is. His free hand starts to move towards my groin and he tries to get his hand down the front of my slacks and then gets frustrated. He slaps me across my face and it burns.

I'm barely conscious.

My last thoughts before I passed out were of Andrew and how he'd be upset to find me like this and how I'd been tarnished and wouldn't be good enough for him. He's such a catch. Who would want someone who's been used and abused?

ANDREW

I arrive at Grace's work. It's 8:45pm and I'm a little early. I think it's because I'm also a little nervous. I have planned a very relaxing night for us. Dinner - she wants Italian - and perhaps a walk along the water's edge. I want to tell her that I like her, not just as a friend, and that I'd like very much if she and I could be a couple. I have butterflies. I pace back and forth. I can't contain my excitement and so I text her – *What time are you finishing? If you're running behind, can I help?*

After several minutes, nothing. 'That's odd, no reply,' I said to myself, so I try to phone her thinking that she might be busy and can't hear the text arriving. Still nothing. That's not like her. She always responds quickly.

I begin to worry. I phone her again. What if something was wrong? Maybe that guy… I start to pace outside the building. My instincts tell me something is wrong. I phone Directory Assistance and ask for Halstead Holdings.

I dial the after-hours number and get put through to Security. I explain the situation and they give me the code to the front. The doors open. The guard tells me that the CCTV did show a man going down in the lift, but that he hasn't left the building. He advised he would call the Police. I thank him and decide to take the stairs.

I just know something is wrong. I can feel it in my gut.

The basement is dark except for the faint emergency lighting.

I don't know the layout. I stop and listen.

I hear a voice. "Cry all you want, scream as loud as you want, but no one can hear you." It's a man's voice, probably the guy from Level 7. I hear Grace crying, gasping for air, then I hear skin being slapped. I want to run in there, but I creep silently towards the room because he might hurt her more if I barge in there.

Grace is gasping more quickly and she screams. What the hell is he doing to her? I don't hear her anymore. I can't wait for backup. I have to save her.

GRACE

"Please stop!" He takes my breast in his mouth again and bites it and leans against me, and his erection is more prominent now. He uses his free hand again to search the front of my slacks, but can't get his hand down the front and gets angry and then goes to the back, and there he gets frustrated by another button which he savagely rips and it pops like the shirt did. It hurts across my waist. He pulls on the zipper. The slacks fall down to the floor. I whimper as he yanks off my underwear and he leans against me and licks my face. I can feel him. I'm naked from the waist down.

My tears are flowing down my face.

He moves closer and tells me, "Put your fucking legs around my waist or I'll hurt you." I comply. I can't breathe, he's suffocating me, and with each attempted breath my lungs burn. I'm not going to be able to remain conscious and perhaps it will be a good thing... to not feel or see what he is doing to me.

He takes his hand away from my face and places two fingers over my wet lips. I scream and squirm. He moves in and out and says crude things in my ear. He tells me I'm wet and I want him. I tell him I don't.

He takes his shaft in his hand and rubs it against my pubic hair and my clitoris, trying to find what he calls my 'tunnel of love.'" I scream as he pushes against me. It hurts. "Ah, you're a fucking virgin! Oh well, it's just gonna hurt you a bit more, bitch."

He's going to rip me open soon. I can feel it with each thrust, and he laughs and says, "Cry all you want, scream as loud as you want, but no one can hear you."

It hurts and he pushes again and I cry out in pain and then, as I fade into unconsciousness, he slaps me and I come to a little.

I try to move away while he is distracted, but he slams my head hard against the wall and I hit the cold hard concrete floor. I think I see a light at the door and I try to crawl towards it, try to stand. I can't see who it is and quite frankly I don't care anymore as my vision swims and the lights go out in my brain and I fall to the ground. I think I'm going to die.

ANDREW

My torch shines on him. I tell him, "Get off her," and he sneers at me. "I'm a police officer." I grab him from behind and he stops pushing against her. He lets her go. She tries to get up, now on her side and eventually to her knees, and she tries to stand but falls to the floor and I hear her head smack sickeningly against the ground and for a second she's still with me, but then she passes out. His pants are undone and his erection is obvious.

"Put your hands on the wall, spread your legs." He then says, "That's what I told this bitch, fucking virgin." He spits at her.

I look at Grace. She's a virgin? I get distracted thinking about her and wanting to hold her. She's naked except for her blouse. My instincts are that I want to cover her up and keep her dignity intact. I search him. "Now back up nice and slow." I make him take his belt off and tie his hands together behind his back. I attach him to a bench so that he can't move. I go over to Grace and get her a fire blanket and drape it over her body.

The lift dings and more police emerge and the lights go on. I tell them we need an ambulance and that they can take that guy away.

Grace is taken to the hospital. There would be time enough for us to give our statements once she is better. I nervously wait outside and when she is finished with the doctor, they let me see her and she tells me, "He didn't… you know…" I say, "I know," and she nods and her face goes red again. I hug her and tell her that he won't hurt her ever again. I kiss her head.

I eventually go home, just as her parents arrive.

The next day after my shift, I went in to see her and her parents arrived shortly after and so I let them have time with her, but they still looked worried. I told them that she's looking better and they seem relieved. The doctor goes in with them. I walk to the waiting room and wait to see what they say, but, something happens that I wasn't expecting.

Her father comes out and talks to me. "She doesn't want to go home with us. She wants to talk to you, son." I stand there perplexed.

I go into the room. I look at her tear-stained face and take her hand in mine. It's as if no one else is in the room but the two of us. That happens a lot around her. I look into her beautiful green eyes and ask what's wrong.

"I want to have dinner with you like we planned," she says. I shake my head and say, "I don't think that's a good idea, you've just been to hell and back, and I think your parents would like to have you home safe in your own bed."

I looked at them both and they nodded.

Grace shakes her head at me. "No, I'm not ready to go home. This was meant to be our first real date and I want to have dinner with you."

I turn around towards her parents and they both raise their shoulders, not knowing what to do or say. I silently plead with them, but she's so stubborn.

Grace starts to cry and so I tell her, "Okay, we'll go have dinner."

She smiles at me through her tears. Her parents say their farewells and I tell them I'll bring her home after we've eaten.

They nod and kiss her on the forehead. We are alone at last.

CHAPTER FIVE

Meet my Mother

ANDREW

"So, where do you want to go?" I ask and she just floors me and says, "To your place."

"Am I hearing things, Grace? Did you just say – my place? You know I live with my mother?" I actually find that I'm blushing.

She looks at me and nods.

I go to leave the cubicle so that she can get dressed. Her parents left some clothes for her. I could hear her saying, "Ouch," while she was trying to get dressed. She's obviously still in pain in places. I want to go in there and help her, but I respect her privacy.

She calls out to me and tells me she is ready. I open the curtain and there she is sitting on the side of the bed. I help her off the bed and grab her hand and slowly we walk to the nurses' station and sign her out and then we walk hand in hand to my car.

I drive home. Lots of thoughts are running through my head. What will my mother say? Do I try to sneak her in and keep Grace locked up in my room all night? Why does she want to go to my place? With any luck, my mother's out or fast asleep.

We arrive at my house and I get out and walk around the car and open her door. I close the door silently and hold her hand in mine and walk up to the front door. The porch light is on. My heart flutters.

I open the door. My mother is awake and is shocked to see me with Grace. My mother's eyes have a million questions.

She smiles.

"Aah, Mum, this is Grace and aah, Grace, this is my Mum." I feel like a teenager and I think I'm in trouble. Maybe it is time I got my own place?

"Hello Grace," she says and looks at me. Mum gets up out of bed and puts on her dressing gown.

I take Grace to the kitchen and start making some macaroni and Mum puts the kettle on.

She sits opposite Grace and eyes her.

We eat, not talking much.

Mum asks, "How was your dinner the other night?"

Grace begins to cry.

I look up at my Mum with imploring eyes and go to Grace and give her a hug. "Please don't cry Grace, you're here with me, it's okay baby."

I get up and carry her to my room and lay her gently on my bed and then I go back to the kitchen and tell Mum what happened.

Mum is shocked and worrying about Grace. "Why didn't she go home with her parents?" she asks.

"I don't know Mum, she said she wanted to have dinner with me and wouldn't take no for an answer. Her parents said okay. I think they just want her to be happy and I guess I make her happy." I shrug.

"I'm going to check up on her. You go back to bed Mum. I'll sleep on the couch if she stays, but I think I'll be driving her home later, if of course she wants to go home."

"Of course, Andrew, if there is anything I can do for her… perhaps she needs a mother's hug too." I say thanks and give her a kiss on the cheek.

I get up and leave Mum in the kitchen and open my bedroom door quietly. Grace is curled up on my bed looking out the window, shaking and crying. I pull my doona over her.

I walk around to her side of the bed. Wow, 'her side of the bed…' It feels like it's been her side for ever and I'm thrilled to feel that way as I kneel down, stroking her arm, concerned. "Do you want to go home, Grace?" She looks up at me with tears in her eyes and shakes her head.

"Okay, you don't have to do anything unless you want to. I'll text your parents and let them know you'll be staying here, okay." I put her phone down after I sent the message and kneel down beside her again.

"Hold me," she says finally.

I climb in behind her and hold her. We sleep in each other's arms all night. I don't let her go. I want to protect her. I want to… what do I want? Well, my subconscious knows what it wants to do. It wants to kiss her all over, feel her skin, and run my fingers through her beautiful auburn hair. It wants to smother her with hugs and make love to her.

But, my brain overrides my subconscious and makes the decision that I would do no such thing to her, even if I really want to. She's had an awful shock and is in pain both emotionally and physically.

During the night, Grace rolls over towards me and snuggles her head underneath my chin and I kiss her head. She opens her eyes and looks at me.

I ask her if she's still in pain and she nods. Grace surprises me again by getting up off the bed and turning the bedside light on. She's wearing a t-shirt and sweatpants.

She says, "Look," and begins to lift up her t-shirt. I stand before her and slide her t-shirt and see all the bruises on her neck, shoulders, and lift it up so I can see her back. Her stomach and even her arms are covered. I take her into my arms again and tell her they will fade.

I fall back onto the bed and she climbs in beside me, and within minutes I can hear her steady breath against my chest and I wrap my arms around her again and fall asleep, our legs entwined. I think I never want to let her go. I think I like her way too much.

It's too soon to feel this way, but there is something about her that just keeps me wanting her more. It's like there's a line tethering us and if we stray too far we'll be pulled back into each other's embrace.

GRACE

I had my reasons for wanting to go to his place. Firstly, I wanted to have dinner with him. What had happened that night at work had ruined our plans for our first official date and I was determined to hear what he wanted to say to me and kiss him and be as happy as can be in his arms, I knew I would be.

The second reason was that I didn't want to go home. The longer I worked and the older I got and the more time I spent with Andrew, the less I actually felt like home was "'home'," if you can understand that. I thought I should be looking for my own place.

I love my family but, I don't know... I just felt it was time.

There was a third reason, but even as I think on it I blush deep, deep inside. I wanted to meet his mother. I wanted to be accepted. I felt a strong desire to be embraced and welcomed by those whom Andrew loves and respects.

He looks at me as he sits down beside my hospital bed and I tell him what I want to do and he is determined that I should go home with my parents but I remain stubborn as always and I know he will give in, and he does.

In the car park, he stops at his car and turns around to me and as he leans towards the door to open it for me, I put my arms around his waist. He holds me and kisses my head. He lingers and I sense he is wanting more. That's what that talk was about. I think he wants me to be his girlfriend but I will wait until he tells me.

"What's this for?" he asks me softly against my forehead.

"I missed you. I don't want to be alone and please let me hang out with you. We never talked at dinner the other night and what you were going to say to me has been playing on my over-active imaginative mind. It scares me and excites me and I guess I wanted to have dinner with you tonight and then if the moment is right we could have that talk?"

I hold him tighter, burying my head against his chest, and take in a deep breath of him and I smile and sigh loudly, content and happy.

He pulls away from me and rubs his thumb over the tear that has escaped my eye and wipes it away.

"We'll have that talk when the time is right, baby."

He opens the car door and helps me inside. He gets in and helps me with my seatbelt and keeps my hand in his all the way to his mother's place.

When we pull up, it looks like an old terrace house. It is painted green and looks pretty.

I think Andrew is nervous.

CHAPTER SIX

Kissing

GRACE

I turn around in bed and open my eyes. They feel heavy and it takes a few moments for them to focus. I immediately think, 'Where am I?' I turn around and beside me is Mr Perfect. It all comes back to me, the events of the other night. I want to touch him, rub my fingers through his hair, and kiss him. He's so beautiful.

I get up carefully, trying not to wake him.

I go out into the hall to the bathroom and relieve myself and then I walk down the stairs, just one at a time because I'm stiff and sore. Andrew's mother is in the kitchen. She smiles and asks me if I'd like a cuppa. I nod and say, "Coffee please." I sit down at the kitchen bench and smile shyly.

"Did you sleep well, dear?" she asks.

"Yes thank you, Mrs Jennings, actually, it's the first night in a long time I've slept so soundly." I think it's because of Andrew being with me, I ponder that thought. "I'm sorry about last night and causing you all to be worried and especially for causing so much trouble, and Andrew…"

"Hey, don't you start apologising Grace, it wasn't your fault, none of it. That creep will have his day in court and you never have to say you're sorry." Andrew holds me close to his chest and kisses my head.

"Listen to my son dear, he knows what he's talking about. You are most welcome here any time you want. In fact, I insist on it. Now eat." 'So that's where he gets his bossiness from,' I mused.

I get up out of my chair, albeit a bit awkwardly, and walk around to the stove and give Andrew's mother a hug. She looks down on me at first with a start and then she smiles and hugs me back. I whisper into her ear, "I like your son, Mrs Jennings, I hope you don't mind. I might take you up on your offer." I stand back at arm's length and she smiles at me and nods and says, "It's about time he had a girlfriend." I blush.

Andrew stands there with a curious expression on his face and a slight smirk. I know he is dying to hear what we said to each other, but I'm not going to tell him and I think his mum won't either.

I eat breakfast with a flourish and ask if I can have a shower.

His mother says she's going up the road to get more groceries and leaves us alone, I think on purpose.

Andrew looks at me and smiles. "I'll get a towel out for you and a change of clothes and I'll leave you to it." We walk up the stairs slowly. He holds my hand and then walks me along the hallway. He opens up a closet and hands me a nice soft blue towel. He steps back as I walk inside the bathroom.

"Kiss me," I say.

Andrew looks at me and his eyebrows gather into a frown in what I've come to know is his concerned face.

"Kiss me," I plead.

"Are you sure?" he asks quietly.

I nod.

"Please don't make me beg you again, Andrew, I need this. I want this."

Andrew leans in and closes his eyes, and I place my two hands on either side of his face and guide it towards mine. Our lips meet and he opens his mouth slightly and moans and I respond by opening up my mouth. I want to explore his mouth, taste him, and my tongue entwines his and he responds in kind. He places his arms around me but doesn't pull me closer. He releases me after a few moments and looks into my eyes. He smiles again and rubs my cheek and lips with his knuckles, savouring the moment.

Our first kiss.

He goes to say something… but he just touches my lips with his thumb. He takes a deep breath and tells me to have my shower.

He looks at me again, his eyes never leaving mine, and kisses me again. I put my arms around him and suddenly I want to shower with him. Touch him, feel him, make wild passionate love to him.

But he squeezes my hands and walks out, closing the door. A gentleman through and through. I sigh.

ANDREW

I wake up and find that Grace is not in bed beside me. I've got a hard-on. Wow, that's not happened for a while. It must be because I'm thinking of her. I smile. It must be late in the morning because the sun is shining through my window. I get up and hear Grace walking down the stairs. I walk down the hall and quickly take the stairs, and I hear Grace talking as I enter the kitchen. Grace is saying, "Yes, thank you, Mrs Jennings. I'm sorry about last night and causing you all to be worried, and especially for causing so much trouble, and Andrew… "

I walk up behind her and shake my head. I have to make her believe it's not her fault. I respond by saying, "Hey, don't you start apologising, Grace, it wasn't your fault, none of it. That creep will have his day in court and you never have to say you're sorry." I hold her and kiss her head. I close my eyes for a second and my mother tells Grace to believe me. Her smell is driving me crazy. Her hair is so soft and I want more. What do I want?

I appreciate my mother's support; it means a lot to me. She even told Grace she could stay here whenever she wanted to, and for that I'm grateful.

Grace gets up off her seat, she teeters for a second and I steady her and she walks over to my mother and gives her a hug. Mum is shocked but soon enough she responds to her and gives her a hug back. They speak quietly; I can't quite hear, which is annoying.

Grace announces she'd like to have a shower and my mother says she's going out. I give her a look and she smiles at me. I am pretty sure she is giving us some privacy.

I'm not going to be anything but a gentleman. I was brought up better than that creep from the other night.

I show Grace to the bathroom and hand her a fresh towel and then she looks at me with something in her eyes that makes me feel a little turned on. Who am I kidding? I'm very turned on.

She asks me to kiss her.

I swallow. Unsure of what to do, I look at her and she's amazing, beautiful, and strong.

She says, "Kiss me," with more emphasis.

I ask her if she's sure. My voice cracks a little because I desperately want to feel her lips on mine and to hold her in an embrace forever and protect her.

Then she says, "Please don't make me beg you again, Andrew, I need this."

I lean in towards her, my eyes never leaving hers. I move my right hand towards her hair and run my fingers through it. Her hair feels so soft. My left hand moves to her lower jaw and her hands go to either side of my face, feeling the beginnings of my beard. 'Which reminds me, I'll have to shave soon,' I thought to myself.

I close my eyes and our lips meet and electricity pulses through my body. It's like we are live wires. She pushes her tongue through my lips and teeth and I do the same after a moment's hesitation. I can taste her and she tastes so fine. I place my arms around her and feel her back and her hips. I don't push up against her, even though I want to. I'm feeling things that I haven't felt before.

My shaft is straining against my pyjama bottoms, but I don't give in to it.

I let her go and look into her beautiful green eyes. I want to tell her to come to bed with me but I refrain. I can't help but smile at her and, when she returns the smile, I feel this need to touch her lips and so I lift my hand up and rub her lips with my thumb, savouring the moment. I breathe again, not realising I had stopped.

"Go have your shower, Grace. I'll see you when you get out. I mean, I'll see you downstairs, then, I'll drive you home."

Her face is flushed and her desire is matching mine. I feel the urge to kiss her again and so I do. She puts her arms around my neck and walks me back toward the shower screen.

Her eyes turn to me, smouldering. I know what she wants. I want it too, but I squeeze her hands and take them from around my neck and walk out and close the door behind me.

The shower turns on and I breathe again. I walk to my room to get my clothes out and notice my face is red and I get her a fresh pair of sweatpants and a t-shirt and some of my underwear to wear.

My mother returns with some groceries and I rush to help her through the door and start putting them away.

The shower stops. I look at my mother.

She looks at me and smiles. My face goes red again.

"You like her, don't you, Andrew?" she asks.

I nod. "A lot, actually."

I wait till Grace is fully dressed and then head off to have my shower. I'm rock hard from kissing her. God, what power does she have over me? I take hold of my shaft and work it, work it, and the thoughts running through my head are about Grace, running my fingers through her auburn hair, kissing her all over.

There's a knock on the bathroom door.

I let go of myself reluctantly. I stick my head out of the shower curtain, thinking it's my mother.

It's Grace! My shaft responds instantly and lets me know it wants me to continue my ministrations.

"Can I come in for a second? I want to brush my teeth. Your mother bought me a toothbrush. I promise I won't look at you, or would you prefer that I waited till later?" she said with a mischievous sparkle in her eye.

The first thing that comes into my mind is that I should open up the shower curtain and let her see all of me and she would give me a blowjob or better still get naked and join me, and then I thought I should tell her, 'Can you wait till after?' but my mouth says, "Sure, come on in, I won't be long."

What was I thinking? Here I am standing completely naked with a hard-on and the girl, oh the woman, I want to – what do I want? I want to drag her into the shower with me and take her clothes off and rub her with soap all over her body and kiss her and make her come.

I get the soap and begin washing my shoulders, face, arms, and chest, and as I work my way down to my legs and feet, I begin to rub the soap over my erect shaft. I start feeling like I'm being watched.

I turn my head.

Grace is staring at me, fully aware of my erection and she can't take her eyes off it. I smile and try to retrieve some dignity. She goes red and walks out into the hallway.

For a second I thought she was going to pull back the curtain and join me like I had imagined earlier. My erection intensifies. I really wanted her to do that, to get on her knees and suck me until I came all over her.

I have to get rid of it. I use the soap and get a rich thick lather going and work it again. I feel relief as I let go and I squirt all over the place, but in my mind's eye I'm squirting over her breasts and then again inside her mouth.

Oh... I've got to stop thinking of her like that. For God's sake, she's just been attacked and nearly raped. I'm chastising myself for my fantasy. Is it going to be like this every time she stays over? Either I'll have to move out really soon so I can have my way with her, or we must have separate rooms, or I can sleep on the couch, and definitely no bathroom sharing.

I step out of the shower and dry myself off and get dressed.

I walk down to the kitchen and eat my breakfast and go back to brush my teeth.

Grace is in the lounge room downstairs talking to my mother. She looks up at me and smiles shyly. I shake my head and tell Mum that I'm going to drive Grace home.

Mum stands up and gives Grace a hug and tells her not to be a stranger.

We walk out to my car, hand in hand.

GRACE

I knock on the bathroom door and slowly open it, revealing a room full of steam.

He's in the shower, naked. He's grunting.

He sticks his head from behind the curtain. He looks like he's been caught with his hand in the cookie jar.

I ask him if I can brush my teeth. His mother had got me a tooth brush, and for a second I think he's going to tell me to go away but he smiles and says I can.

Whilst I brush, he looks at me and then closes the curtain again and uses the soap all over his gorgeous body. I want to rub soap on his body – all over – especially on his shaft. I look at myself in the mirror and see that I'm blushing again and there is a weird feeling between my legs. I want him.

I open up the shower curtain. He's turned away from me and then turns and looks at me and realises he's holding it and turns away again and I want to touch it. Feel it. Rub it on me and suck it and have it inside me, but I walk away. I don't know what's come over me.

I've never felt this way before and quite frankly it terrifies me. What was he thinking of to get so aroused? My subconscious says, 'You.' I stop dead outside the door.

I hear him grunting again and then I hear a moan which sends shivers down my spine and I know he has found his release. I want to hear that moan when he's on top of me. My nipples harden.

I head down to the lounge room to distract myself. His mother is watching something and so we start to talk and get to know each other better.

He comes down the stairs and gets his breakfast and doesn't look at me and then goes back upstairs and then comes down again. This time our eyes meet. He goes slightly red and smiles and he tells his mother he's going to drive me home.

I get a hug from his mother and then he takes my hand, and my heart, as we walk out to his car.

"I hope you didn't mind me brushing my teeth before. I should have waited till you were finished. I apologise also for being so rude as to ogle at you when you were washing yourself."

My eyes are downcast but he says to me, "It was okay, Grace. We're a couple now and as such we will eventually be more comfortable in each other's company. It's just that I wasn't expecting you to be at the door and I think that, because I live with my mother, we should respect her and be more controlled with our feelings and actions," and not for the first time, I think that I should move out of my parent's place.

"Thanks Andrew, I'm so relieved that you are okay with this and I promise I'll be conscious of your wishes and your mother's from now on." And I think to myself, 'If only I could control my hormones.'

We drive down the Princes Highway.

We're both quiet, thinking our own thoughts, and after a while I doze off with the warm sun on me. I feel cosy and then I wake up and I plead with him to pull over at the park because I have to get out. Suddenly, everything hits me and I feel so claustrophobic and I can't breathe!

He's out of the car within seconds and follows me, but he doesn't touch me.

I'm not breathing. My eyes open in panic and I turn to him and collapse in his arms again.

I can't breathe and he sits me up and tells me to breathe into my hands so I cup them around my mouth and nose. He says, "That's it. Try to breathe slowly, baby." He called me 'baby' again! I like him so much. I breathe in and out, never taking my eyes off his, which are full of concern for me, real concern.

I think I'm scaring him, heck I'm scared myself. I've never hyperventilated before. One minute I'm holding his hand resting on my lap and the next second my mind starts to wander to the what-ifs. What if Andrew hadn't turned up when he did? What if that man had raped me? What if he'd killed me? I couldn't breathe because he suffocated me, with his arm strangling me, across my throat.

After a while, I start to breathe normally again and he smiles at me. I take my hands away from my mouth and tears start, and he rubs his thumb down my cheek and then holds me close. I'm sitting on his lap and he is rocking me gently back and forth like my father used to.

He lifts my head up to his and kisses me, deeply and passionately, and says, "I think I should get you home now." His eyes look sad.

I nod and he lifts me up and we walk back to the car.

He doesn't ask me what I dreamt, he just holds my hand close to him and takes me home in silence.

ANDREW

One minute I look over at the most beautiful woman I've ever laid eyes on and she's asleep in my car and I'm holding her hand as it rests on her thigh, her head resting against the door, and the next second she's screaming at me to pull over. At first I thought she was going to be sick and so I pull over, but she gets out of the car and runs. I get out and run towards her. I don't know what to do.

She grabs her throat and she can't breathe. Her face goes a deathly shade of white and her lips begin to turn a light shade of grey. She collapses to her knees but I grab her and hold her. It's then that I realise she's hyperventilating and so I tell her what to do. After a tense ten minutes or so she starts to calm down. I'm scared. She's really freaked me out. I have to get her home. She's exhausted and very emotional and probably needs a few hours of TLC from her own mother.

I smile at her and rub the tears on her cheek away and give her a hug. I rock her like my mother used to do as it soothes us both and I lift her head and kiss her, kiss her for all the feelings I have deep inside. I like this woman very much. I tell her that I'm going to take her home and she nods.

We sit in silence but it's okay. I never let go of her hand and it seems to provide assurance to her that I'm not going to disappear or leave her.

After she closes the front door, I sit in the car and realise I'm crying too. I wipe the tears away and drive off. I feel so angry and when I go back to work tonight I'm going to give my statement and hopefully that creep will not be given bail and will be put away for a very long time.

I was a witness to the assault, so he hasn't got a hope in hell between that and Grace's testimony.

When I got home, I went straight up to my room and got ready for work. I'm on nights, so I go and have a nap.

I wake up at about 9pm and to my surprise there is a text from Grace. I wasn't expecting one considering everything that happened in the last forty eight hours.

Dear Mr Perfect,

I smile because that was the first name she called me and it brings back fond memories.

I cannot see you anymore. I realised on the way home and in the park that I'm no good for you. You deserve a girl friend who doesn't have drama in her life, someone who can give you a normal life. I've caused you to worry since the moment I met you and I saw it in your eyes at the park. I scare you.

Please forget me. I really need to be by myself from now on and I do hope you understand that I cannot continue to see you. The feelings I was beginning to have for you, well let's just say I don't want to have them anymore. If you know what's good for you, you'll forget me.

Yours no more, Grace

I sit on the side of my bed in shock. I run through the text again and again and realise that yes, I was scared this afternoon, not of her but of the fact that she was in distress. I have to talk to her and straighten it out. I don't want to lose her.

I go have my shower and get dressed for work.

It's obvious that I'm distracted and Gerry asks me what's wrong.

I motion with my head to the tearoom and tell him everything and he nods and says that I have to talk to her. He suggests we go for a drive. I say to him, "But that's not our area. We can't just turn up; she'll think I'm stalking her."

Gerry takes my shoulders in his hands and stands in front of me. "Andrew, think of it this way. She got attacked and nearly raped three nights ago in that very building; do you think she'll be okay in there on her own?" I slowly understand his meaning and he says, "C'mon, we'll tell the Captain we're doing a follow-up. She might be able to give us her statement too if she's okay."

And just like that we take the police car to St James and I text from outside the building.

There is no answer. I look at Gerry and he says, "You've still got the code? Use it."

I nod and punch in the code and the doors open and we walk inside with our torches on.

I press the Down button to the basement and Gerry waits in the foyer in case Security enquires.

I get to the basement and the doors open with a 'ding'. I remember the last time I was in the basement and the noises I'd heard. This time I hear only sobbing. I walk to the cleaner's room and sure enough Grace is down on the floor crying.

I get onto my radio with Gerry. "She's down in the basement." Gerry says, "Okay, I'll meet you outside at the car."

I say, "Over and out," and walk towards her. She is lying on the floor in the foetal position and I grab her bag, scoop her up in my arms, and hold her to my chest.

I press the lift button and take her up to the foyer.

I put her into the back of the car and Gerry drives her to the station. I sit with her in the back, holding her close.

The Captain looks at me as I carry her inside and nods to the right and then walks ahead of me and opens up the door to the tearoom. I carry her in and put her down on a chair gently and Gerry makes her a cup of coffee and hands me a box of tissues.

I wipe her tears and we sit down at the table, just the three of us, and wait for her to calm down enough to talk to us.

GRACE

I've hurt him so much. I can see it in his eyes. He hesitates and, although he is hugging me and kissing me and telling me to breathe, I know he is sad. I'm no good for him.

When I got home, I went up to my bedroom, glad that my parents were still out. I slept for a few hours and when I woke up I texted him and told him I couldn't see him anymore and that he'd be better off without me. I feel like I've just raked my heart through broken glass and torn it to shreds.

I go have a bath and clean myself down there, again trying to get rid of that man and his smell and feel, and I rub myself raw. I get dressed and head off to work. 'I can do this,' I keep saying to myself, 'I can go to each floor and clean and then go home and it'll be easy. I can do this. I'm a strong independent woman and I can do this.'

I tell myself this over and over, until I think I actually believe it.

On Level 7 I note that that man's office is empty and cleaned out completely. That helps. I had to report the incident to HR here, which was difficult when I was coming into work. Andrew advised HR when I had been in hospital on my behalf, so all was okay with them. I had my dinner on Level 5 and then cleaned my way down to the foyer.

I got to the basement and put the trolley close to my room and started to repack it for tomorrow night. When I finish, I leave it by the lift as per usual. I go back into the room and begin to get changed. I undo my overall buttons and step out of it and then my mind goes into panic mode as I hear a sound… somewhere… and my mind goes back in detail to the last night I was in this room.

I instinctively run to the shelf and grab a torch to use in case the lights go out, and I look around for a weapon and I grab a mop.

When after a long time no one appears and the lights are still on, I see a rat running through the rubbish waiting to be taken up to the street... and that rat was the sound I had heard previously. I collapse, as much with relief as shock.

I curl up in a ball and cry and cry, and then out of nowhere I feel strong, familiar arms around me. I'm being lifted and held and it smells like Andrew, my Mr Perfect, but it can't be him because I told him to leave me as I was no good for him.

He takes me up in the lift and kisses my head and tells me everything will be okay and that he's here now and walks me to a car and puts me inside and shuts the door. The car purrs and the next thing I know I'm in his arms again and being carried into the police station and put onto a seat in a kitchen.

A cup of coffee is placed next to me. A jacket is placed onto my shoulders and I'm shivering and shaking and crying and somewhere people are talking. My brain is not coherent. I can't make anything out. I feel like I'm in a well or on a fluffy cloud looking down upon the room. It's surreal.

Andrew hands me the coffee and I think he wants me to drink it, but I just don't move. He shakes his head and looks up at someone standing behind me. He gets up and leaves me alone with a woman in a police uniform, who sits with me and smiles.

I don't register.

It's like I've had a stroke and my brain is working but I just can't do anything; I'm a vegetable, devoid of any feeling.

The policewoman talks to me.

"You've been through a very difficult couple of days, Grace." How does she know my name? "I want you to tell me what happened and what you were feeling and thinking yesterday and then tonight when you were at work. Can you do that for me?"

The only word I can utter is "Perfect," barely audibly, and she leans in towards me, confused. "Did you say perfect?" I say it again, "Perfect."

The policewoman rises and goes out to the front desk. She talks to someone and then Andrew comes in with her and leans in towards me, his eyes intense and with hope in them.

"Grace, it's me, Mr Perfect." The policewoman smiles at him and laughs. I guess it is funny, but it was my first name for him.

"I'm here for you, baby and I'm not going anywhere." The policewoman begins to get up and says to him, "I think the two of you need a moment alone." Andrew, without looking away from me says, "Thanks," and out she goes.

"Kiss me," I tell him, and this time he does. He plants a kiss on my trembling lips.

"Kiss me harder," I say to him, and he kisses me like we kissed at the park, passionately, and our tongues are blazing and searching the depths.

I pull my head away and my eyes begin to focus.

"Don't leave me. Never ever leave me again. I was wrong, I need you. I'm being so very selfish asking this of you, but I think I'm in love with you and I'm scared."

ANDREW

I walk outside and leave Constable Naylor alone with Grace in the tearoom. I don't want to leave her but it's what's best for her. Maybe she'll talk to another woman?

A short while later the door opens and Constable Naylor asks, "Do you know who or what 'perfect' means?"

I go inside and sit down by her. Constable Naylor smiles and laughs when I tell Grace that it's me, I'm Mr Perfect. I'm staring at her and I think Constable Naylor feels a little embarrassed as I call Grace 'baby' and so leaves us alone.

Grace says, oh so quietly, "Kiss me," and this time I do it without hesitation.

"Kiss me harder," she says and I do it just like we did at the park. Oh, that kiss… I'll remember it forever.

My heart breaks when Grace looks at me and asks me, begs me, to never leave her and I promise her I won't. I try to tell her it doesn't matter, what she said in the text. I knew she was just worrying about me and I tell her she is anything but selfish and then she comes out with a bombshell.

"I think I'm in love with you."

I don't know what to say. I feel very strongly for her, but is it love? I've never been in love before. I have to think about all of this.

I hold her closer and she shifts herself onto my lap.

The door opens and the Captain tells me to leave while he and Gerry take her statement and he assures Grace that I will be just outside and they try again to understand just what is going on inside Grace's head.

I leave the door open a crack and listen to her tell Gerry and the Captain exactly what happened again and Gerry takes her statement and I can see it all in my mind's eye as she gets to the part where I walked in on him. She continues to explain what happened in the car on the way home from my place.

It explained a lot. She was having a nightmare and had repressed the feelings about it, but like all things it was poking its ugly head through to be let out.

Then she explained what happened down in the basement, with me once again walking in to find her on the floor, and then how she was for the whole time she was here until moments ago. She sounded better and I felt that by telling us everything she was thinking and feeling, she would be on her way to healing.

I walked back into the room and Grace turns to me and says, "I want to go." I look at the Captain and he nods and says, "It's nearly the end of your shift anyway; the other guys are changing in the locker room. Off you go."

GRACE

Andrew walks me out to his car and opens the car door and makes sure I am strapped in and safe. He gets in on the driver's side and reverses out of the driveway.

We drive towards the Prince's Highway. I say to him, "Not Jannali." He looks at me and says, "Where then?"

I look at him and say, "St Peters."

He turns down a side-street and within moments we're pulling up outside his place. I open the car door and get out without his help.

He takes my hand and I follow him inside.

His mother is in bed reading. She looks up from her book and smiles. "Is everything alright, darling?" she asks as we walk inside, and Andrew replies with a yes. I head for the stairs and Andrew follows me.

I ask him if I could have a bath and he says, "Sure, here's a clean towel and I'll leave a pair of clean underwear and some tracksuit pants and a t-shirt out for you." Maybe I should bring some of my stuff here? I will have to ask Andrew if that is okay.

I thanked him and went inside to run the bath.

I wanted it very hot, almost scalding. I felt so unclean and I wanted to make sure that that man, my attacker, was washed clean off me. I wanted to feel normal again. I was sick and tired of jumping at shadows and feeling dirty, and this would help me heal.

I was scrubbing myself on my arms, legs, and chest, everywhere he touched me.

It became a ritual for me now. Andrew came into the bathroom and grabbed my hands. He said, "You're bleeding, stop! What are you doing to yourself?" He pulled the plug and stood me up. He saw my thighs and groin were smeared with my blood.

A few seconds later Andrew wraps a towel around me and lays me on his bed and then he goes downstairs and returns with bandages and some antiseptic from the kitchen cupboard.

"Baby, what did you do to yourself?" He looks at my arms and legs. He asks permission to look at the bleeding wounds on my chest and I nod. He slowly removes my towel and then looks at my face and tells me he will help me. I think he means with everything, not just this. Does he love me?

"This is going to hurt," he tells me.

He dabs some of the antiseptic on my thighs and it hurts just like he said it would. My arms and chest are also dabbed with antiseptic and I cry out in pain and embarrassment. He looks at my face after he's finished, wrapping the towel around me, and I think he is relaxing a little bit. I was embarrassed. How could I explain that I was just wanting to wash the essence of that man off my body, but he just says, "Hey, don't be embarrassed. It doesn't change anything, not the way that I feel towards you. If anything, it has made me realise just how much I care."

He helped me dress and then got me into his bed. He lay beside me until I had stopped crying and then he left the room. He didn't return to me. I cried some more 'cause I missed him and I'd obviously scared him all over again. Andrew slept downstairs that night.

ANDREW

I went into the bathroom after I knocked a few times, because Grace was in there a very, very long time and I was beginning to worry.

As I go in I see the bathwater the colour of blood and my first thought is that she's slashed her wrists, but then I realise as I get closer that she's raw. Her skin is raw in patches.

I say to her, "You're bleeding, stop! What are you doing to yourself?" I pulled the plug and stood her up. I saw her thighs and everything, but it was far from arousing.

I put a towel around her and I carried her to my room and put her on the bed. I got the first aid kit from down in the kitchen. I looked into her agonised eyes as I began to rub the antiseptic on her thighs and it hurts me to see her raw skin. She cries with the pain, but it has to be done. I ask her if I can remove the towel from around her chest and she says yes, her breasts are raw in places, her nipples are red and sore. I dab the antiseptic where I can, gently, not wanting to cause her any more pain, and then I close the towel around her and her face is red and she's embarrassed. I say to her, "Hey, don't be embarrassed. It doesn't change anything, not the way I feel towards you. If anything, it has made me realise just how much I care."

I hand her the t-shirt and pants and I help her dress. I motioned for her to lie on the bed next to me and she did. I waited for her to calm down and then I left her side. I left the door slightly open and went down stairs. I slept on the couch.

It was agonising for me. I could hear her crying. I wanted to go up to her and comfort her like the last night that she stayed over. Then there was silence.

I thought she must have fallen asleep in exhaustion but I was wrong. Her feet are softly walking down the stairs and she comes into the lounge room. She's wearing the t-shirt and sweat pants.

She does something I didn't expect. She puts her hand in mine and says, "Come." She leads me out the front door and we sit on the front steps at 3am in the morning.

"Why'd you do that to yourself?" I ask her.

"Mr Perfect, I was trying to clean that man off me… everywhere he touched me. I felt dirty and stained and ugly. I just wanted him to be gone." Grace cried into her hands.

I looked out onto the street and sighed and put my arm around her. At least she told me, that was a start. I'd take her home in the morning and tell her parents and that they should take her to get some professional help. There wasn't much I could do for her right now, even though I wanted to be with her every minute of the day and night; she needed professional help.

CHAPTER SEVEN

Home

GRACE

I've decided to surprise him because I haven't seen him for a few weeks as I've been recuperating at home and seeing doctors galore.

I walk through the gate and climb the six steps and gingerly knock on the front door. It's about 2pm and I've still got a few days off before I have to return to work. I hope he's home. I think I can hear his voice in the lounge room but I'm not sure.

There is movement on the other side of the door and he opens it. His shirt is off and he's on the telephone and he looks at me with surprise as a smile slowly spreads across his face. He motions me inside and shuts the door.

I stand in the vestibule and he ends his conversation. I wonder who he's speaking to?

He hangs up the telephone and returns to me saying, "You can come in. I'm not going to bite you." Part of me wishes he would. I smile back at him and go into the lounge room.

"Is your mother home, Andrew?" I ask and he shakes his head. His blue eyes are staring at me with mischief in them and he remembers his manners all of a sudden and asks if I want something to drink.

"No, that's fine I just wanted to say hi."

"Hi," he says and smiles.

He sits down next to me and puts his hand in mine and squeezes it. "I've missed you, Grace," he says, with that crease on his forehead telling me he is concerned.

"I'm fine now, Andrew. No more bloody baths and I'm really looking forward to work next week and seeing you more, that is, if you still want me?" I look up at him shyly, hoping he wants the same thing. That he wants to hold me, love me, and never let me go.

He stands and takes hold of my hand and leads me to the stairs. He looks down at me and stares into my eyes. His eyes remind me of the ocean. I'm not breathing again, only this time it's because he is so beautiful and hot.

He kisses my cheek and whispers into my ear, "Let me show you how much I've missed you and want you... breathe Grace, that's my girl." The emphasis was on the word 'my.' I sigh. He motions his head toward the stairs and I smile and follow him up.

He stops outside his bedroom. I swallow. I look up at him and smile and he opens the door and enters. His window is open, admitting a refreshing breeze, and the bed covers are a blue matching his eyes. He motions for me to come in and then closes the door and locks it behind me.

My heart is racing. My pupils are dilated and I have missed him so much. I want to feel his body beneath my fingers.

He sits on the bed and taps his thigh for me to sit on it. I slowly take a seat on his lap and he wraps his arms around me, his strong protective arms. He cradles me against his chest and tells me, "I've really missed you Grace. So much so that I phoned you every day and you never answered your mobile, but I understood you were not in a good place."

"I had wanted to phone you back, but the therapist said that I should give us some space. And so, here I sit wanting you back to fill in the empty space that's been in my heart since I was last with you."

Andrew turned my face to his and looked, really looked, into my eyes and smiled my special smile and kissed me and I kissed him back and he ran his hand down my neck and then… oh, I was hoping he'd do more and touch me everywhere, but he just grazed my collarbone and let me go.

I just sat there in his arms for what seemed like days. I never wanted to leave him and I think he felt the same way.

ANDREW

"**...** Hmm, someone is at the door, just hold on a second Gerry."
I open it up and to my surprise it's Grace. I motion for her to
come in and I think I'm going to burst with happiness.

"Yeah, I've gotta go now, see you later," without taking my eyes
off hers.

I tell her to come in and we walk into the lounge room and then I
remember I should have offered her a drink, but she doesn't want
anything so we sit. I hold her hand and she tells me she's better.
I want to hold her and caress her and so I take her upstairs.

But before I take the first step, I hold her against me and I stare
down at her beautiful eyes that remind me of emeralds and
summer… maybe my poetry is improving? I lean down to her ear
and say, "Breathe Grace, that's my girl." We start climbing the
stairs.

I can feel her pulse in her hand and she's excited. I want to feel
her heart, place my hand onto her chest, and oh God I'm rock-
hard again. What is she doing to me?

I lock my door and I sit on the bed motioning for her to sit on my
lap. She slides over towards me and I can feel her firm buttocks
and thighs, and I wish she was sitting with both thighs on either
side of my hips… I wish I was inside her.

I told her that I'd really missed her and even owned up to
phoning her every day, but she wasn't allowed to call me back,
which is fine... I get it.

I kiss her. I graze my fingers against her cheek and neck and I really want to tip her back onto my bed and make love to her but I couldn't. I just got her back and I wanted to hold her and never let her go.

We sit like this for… gee, I look out the bedroom window and realise it is almost dinner time. I ask her if she'd like to have dinner with me and she nods.

I go downstairs and fish out some chicken pieces and I get the pan out and start cooking and while they are sizzling I cut up some salad and after a while I put her plate on her lap in the lounge room and we eat in comfortable silence.

I clean up after dinner, with Grace drying the dishes, and then I ask if she'd like me to drive her home?

Grace looks at me seriously and I think something is wrong.

"What is it, Grace?" I ask.

"Can I leave some of my clothes here so that I can stop having to wear your underwear and t-shirts and sweat pants?" she asks and blushes.

"Sure, I can clean out a drawer for you if you'd like." I'm relieved that it was nothing bad, as we'd had enough of that to last us a good while. I kiss her again and each time I do it gets that little bit harder to let her go. My heart swells with a strange feeling. I don't know exactly what it is, all I know is I want to spend the rest of my life with her… oh my God, I think I love her.

I let her go reluctantly and glide my tongue down her jaw and neck and then look back at her eyes; she's happy and that's all I want or need.

The thought that I should move out comes into my mind again when my mother arrives home.

She comes into the kitchen with some groceries and greets us, the spell broken between us by the intrusion. It happens all the time, but we look at each other and it feels like we are all alone in the world, like no one exists except us.

My mother looks at me and motions for me to talk to her in her bedroom. I give Grace a shrug of my shoulders. Grace finishes drying up and puts the groceries away and then meanders to the lounge room.

"I see Grace is back," says my mother.

I can't help smiling. "Yep."

"So, you two are back together, how are things between you two?" She fishes for information.

I take her in my arms and look down at her blue eyes and say, "Mother, can Grace leave a few things here, clothes and stuff, so that when she stays over she can have her own clothes to wear?"

"Of course, Andrew," she replies and she smiles because I think I just answered her question.

She hugs me back and tells me that she will be going to visit her sister in Raven in a few days and that if I want Grace to stay over all the time it was fine with her.

I blush.

"I'll think about it, Mum, but thanks for approving," I say earnestly.

"Andrew, she's a very beautiful young woman and I think she loves you and I think you feel exactly the same way.

You've been seeing each other now for nearly a year, although she was in therapy for a good while, and before that you were becoming friends but you didn't stop caring for her and about her.

I'm surprised you haven't popped the question already." She looks at me hopefully and playfully giggles, jabs me in the ribs, and leaves the room.

I'm flabbergasted. I've not thought about marriage. I only just realised I loved Grace. I should tell her; that would be a start. Again, I think maybe I should move out of home.

My mother goes out to the lounge room and talks to Grace while I just sit on the edge of her bed trying to regain some balance before I take her home. My thoughts glide to spending the rest of my life with Grace.

Moving out together, marriage, and one day kids. I imagine a little auburn-haired version of Grace and I smile. My heart is close to breaking apart because I realise that I love her, I love her with every fibre in my body.

I've never felt this way before and I have to tell her. What has she done to me? My subconscious tells me plainly, 'She loves you, trusts you, wants you.' I want her too, more than anything in my life. I know that now.

I stand up and open the bedroom door. Grace looks at me and tilts her head to the side questioningly. I smile back and say, "I'm going to take you home now, beautiful."

The drive to take her home went way too quickly. A part of me wanted to drive somewhere secluded and make out with her, and I could feel myself succumbing to my need for her body.

I stop outside of her place and broach the question.

"Grace, what would you say if we moved in together, you know, got our own place?" I'm nervous.

Grace looks at me and seems shocked at first, but then she smiles and says, "One day that would be great."

I clear my throat and turn completely to face her and say the words which I want to say. "Grace, I just realised something today… I love you."

Grace smiles and tells me she loves me too and we kiss, long and passionately. Then I realise her little sister is watching us from her window and Grace goes red and says, "The sooner the better," and then gets out of the car.

I chuckle to myself and head home

CHAPTER EIGHT

Firsts

GRACE

I stepped out of the lift on Level 10 to start my shift and there was a woman dressed in a business suit with her hair in a bun and glasses perched on the end of her nose. She looked at me as I excused myself for disrupting her at her desk. It was very rare that staff were here this late.

"Grace, isn't it? Please sit. I've been watching your work here and I am happy to advise since you started that complaints have fallen to zero. It hasn't happened before and quite frankly I'm wondering what you do each night that is so vastly different to all the other janitors we've tried. You have been the one that Mr Bennett felt the most comfortable with.

I sit there and smile. It's pretty good news to hear and I can't wait to tell my folks and Andrew.

"I want to offer you a job as my Personal Assistant. It's quite a bump-up in pay compared to the janitorial role and I think you'll fit in here very well. You're resourceful. Punctual. Dedicated.

All the qualities I want. I need someone to manage everything as I am often away at courses and conferences or at our other offices all over Australia. What do you say?"

I didn't even think about it. Wow, a promotion. I smiled and shook her hand. I was going to be the Personal Assistant to the head of HR.

She said I could have the rest of the night off and come Monday a new person was starting in the role of Janitor and she will be placing them on trial, much like Mr Bennett did with me.

It was 8pm.

I walked to The Rocks police station and went inside. Andrew was there typing something on the computer at the front desk.

"Can we talk privately?" I ask.

He looks up at me and smiles and has a look around and nods.

"I just got told that tonight was my last night as a janitor," I tease and he takes the bait.

"What? They can't fire you, on what grounds?"

"Oh Andrew, I just got a promotion. The head of HR wants me to be her PA! I'm going to get more money and then we can move in together like we were thinking."

He realises I was teasing and gives me a look but then his face changes and he smiles.

"I'm so proud of you," says Andrew.

He hands me a set of keys and tells me to let myself in and he'd be home after 12am.

I kissed him and caught the train from Circular Quay to St Peters and walked to his place. I let myself in and remembered we had the place to ourselves as his mother was visiting a relative.

I left the outside light on for him.

I went to the kitchen and opened up the fridge and made myself some macaroni. I ate it in front of the TV and had a bath with smelly stuff that Andrew loves and then I watched TV on the couch and I must have fallen asleep whilst watching some movie marathon.

ANDREW

I look up and, to my surprise, standing in front of me is the most beautiful woman in the world, and it takes me a second to realise she's all mine. I smile and she tells me she's not going to be a janitor anymore, as of tonight.

I instantly think they've fired her and she doesn't say anything to alert me to any other possibility, and then she smiles and tells me she's got a promotion. I could have spanked her for teasing me like that, but I'm so thrilled for her and hand her my spare keys. I'd been meaning to give them to her for a week but I forgot. She mentions we can move out now. Hmmm... I think I'll start looking for a rental.

I finished my shift at 11pm, headed home with Gerry driving me, and when I got in the front door I heard the TV on. "Surely she's not up this late waiting up for me?" I said to myself. And there's my girl, asleep on the couch with her legs curled up, and she looks so beautiful. I move a strand of her hair away from her face and she stirs.

I go upstairs and have a shower and get changed ready for bed and then I close my window and blinds to make the room dark enough to sleep, turn the TV off, and pick her up and carry her to our bed.

I didn't stop there this time. I actually pulled her slippers and socks off and took her dressing gown from around her shoulders.

She was wearing my t-shirt again and my sweatpants and so I pulled back the doona and climbed in behind her. I looked at her for what felt like hours and found myself falling in love all over again.

I kissed her and she turned around and mumbled something which sounded like hello.

I kissed her again and this time she responded and kissed me back. I said "Hello" back and my arms are around her and she hugs me and kisses me again. I want to go further and so I take it slow and kiss and nibble her earlobe, her jaw and neck, and I look up at her and she nods imperceptibly while I continue my aerial assault on her shoulders and take off her t-shirt.

I open my bedside drawer and pull out a string of condoms for later. I take off my t-shirt next and she kisses the downy hair on my chest and kisses and suckles my nipples, which sends thrills down my spine. I repay the favour and she moans. It sounds heavenly.

I kiss her down to her belly button and Grace squirms beneath me.

I take off my pyjama pants and then hers and her underwear in one continuous move. I lean against her; we are facing each other and our eyes are excited and my God she's sexy and I want her.

Grace giggles and moves with speed down to my shaft and takes me in her mouth. I'm in shock, but it feels divine. With slow strokes up and down and her tongue against my head, I buck and grip the back of her hair and arch my hips up, in time with her downward motion.

I push her gently off me as I think I'm going to cum, but I don't want to, not yet.

I roll her over onto her back and kiss her mouth again and I can taste myself in there and she loves me.

I trail kisses down to her breasts and pull on her nipples with one hand while I suckle her, and then reverse it and she arches her back and grips the bed sheets.

I want to pleasure her and make love to her and I kiss her feet, her ankles, her shins and calves and she is perplexed as I do it, but loving it. I trail my tongue up to her knee and kiss her inner thighs and lightly roll my tongue and nose in her groin, sending electric sparks up her body. I can smell her need. It makes me want her more.

When I got to the lips, I told her to move her knees up and I gently opened her up, exposing her sex to me. I found her clitoris and I licked it and sucked it and blew on it and she writhed. My shaft was straining to be inside her, pulsating in time with her panting breath.

I poked my tongue into her and she moaned and groaned and my God she was wet. I put two fingers inside her, feeling her hymen and the tension against my fingers as I moved them slowly, oh so slowly, in and out and around and around, finding the spot that made her deliciously aroused, my tongue making slow circles around her pussy.

I couldn't wait anymore. I manoeuvred myself on top of her and looked her in the eye and asked the silent question. She smiled and raised her hips so that my shaft was resting between her legs and I put my hand around it and, oh so slowly and gently, eased myself in and instantly felt the tightness and then I pulled back again, never leaving her eyes.

I moved inside her again, her eyes closing and her lips opening with a rush of air, this time I go in further and firmer and I can feel her give a little.

It's agonisingly slow but I have to do it this way with a virgin, because she'd be in pain otherwise.

I moved inside her again and this time she opened up to me and I slid inside. It hurt her a little and she cried out, still looking at me with those wide green eyes, and I kissed her mouth again and pulled out slowly, working into a rhythm back and forth, in and out, and she was beginning to match my pace, her hips rising and falling with each thrust.

I wanted to feel all of her, so I told her to sit on top of me and with each downward thrust I raised my hips and met her and she said breathlessly how she could feel all of me now. "Better penetration baby," I said and before long I knew she was going to cum, so I rolled her over onto her back again and thrust again and again, picking up the pace. I could feel the spasms inside her and, as if on cue, we both came together and I could feel myself squirt again and again deep inside her.

Grace's laboured breathing was all I could hear as I swam in a sea of tranquillity. I rested my head on her breasts while I caught my breath. I kissed her nipples again. She cried and I understood how she felt. It was sheer joy that overflowed from my heart for her.

I realised there and then that she was mine. I knew without a doubt that we were destined to be together for ever and that I loved her with every fibre of my body. I loved her. I wouldn't have had sex with her if I hadn't. It wasn't until a good while later that I pulled out of her and instantly got up to take off the condom, but when I looked down I realised I'd not put it on. I looked at her all snuggled up in the bed falling into a glorious, exhausted sleep. The sheets beneath her were red. The condom was still on the bedside table.

GRACE

I can't believe we made love and I think I'm the happiest I've ever been. I lie in bed next to him and watch him sleep as the sun slowly creeps up to his window announcing it's time to get up. I remembered how it all started, what with him sliding into bed next to me last night… or was it early this morning? He kissed me and I kissed him back and he just was so gentle and told me over and over again that he loved me. I felt so emotional and finally I wanted to give myself to this man whom I loved completely.

He kissed me all over my body and I put his shaft inside my mouth and it felt so good that I can't wait to do that again and he kissed me down there and licked me and sucked me and I thought I was going to die with the pulsating pleasure of his tongue inside me and then, oh then he entered me and he was so gentle at first and I felt myself open like a flower opening up to the sun and he entered me again and again and it felt so good and I just wished I could have taken all of him, but then he moved me on top of him and, oh my, I could feel him and I was in control and I almost lost myself but he moved me around again and this time it was so much more intense.

He thrust his shaft inside me again and again and I felt my heart beat in my chest and I was so wet and he made me cum, so much water and the spasms inside me, and then he pushed inside me deeper than before and I felt him. I didn't even feel the condom, it must have been extra thin, I was so super sensitive.

I was in a bubble of joy and emotional too. All of a sudden I started to weep. It was such an intimate act. Two people having sex. I loved him with all my heart and soul.

How could I not? He was my Mr Perfect and he lay on top of me for a lifetime until our breathing was back to normal. I never wanted him to leave me. The thought of us made me want him again but I had to go to the bathroom first.

I slide out from under his arms and go to the bathroom, noting the sheets. I will have to soak them later.

I stare at myself and I am blissfully happy this morning.

We should definitely find our own place to live, no question now. I can't imagine his mother would appreciate it if I cried out like I did last night when he got me to sit on top of him. I felt him inside me and I'm sore now, but wow.

I return to the bedroom and put on my t-shirt and sweatpants and go down to the kitchen to make breakfast. I think pancakes will do the trick; apparently they're his favourite.

I'm just serving them when sleepyhead walks down the stairs and looks a little lost until he sees me and smiles with relief.

He comes over and kisses me and asks me how I slept and I reply, "Never better, and you?" I looked into his eyes and for just a split second he seemed to be concerned about something and then he said, "Great," but the smile didn't go up to his eyes.

We ate breakfast together and then he cleaned up. I looked at him and suggested we have a bath and he takes my hand and leads me upstairs.

The hot water felt wonderful. After a while he begins to massage my neck and shoulders with the soap and this feels wonderful too. His touch is making me want him all over again and so I turn around and sit on him with my legs on either side of his and he looks at me and shakes his head and says, "I'm not ready yet, perhaps later, babe?"

I feel dejected, rejected. I can feel his almost erection. How can he not be ready?

I got up off him and we got out of the bath and got dressed. A while later he says he will drive me home.

I ask him what is wrong in the car, but he says with a smile, "Nothing baby, I've got another night shift in a few hours, that's all."

Why don't I believe him?

ANDREW

I forgot to use a condom. Shit! I never forget to wear a fucking condom. Fuck!

I walk into the bathroom and have a shower cursing myself under the stream of water. Washing her off my shaft. Chastising myself for being an absolute idiot. Should I tell her? Maybe she's been anticipating this night and is on the pill or maybe it's not that time of the month for her? How will I know if she's on the pill, ask her? Or go through her toiletries or purse?

I came back into my bedroom and looked at her. I asked myself, 'What have I done?'

I pull my hair and resolve to think about it in the morning, but when I wake up she is gone. I get up wondering if she's left or if she was somewhere downstairs.

When I get to the kitchen there she is looking so relaxed and deliriously happy. I haven't seen her look like that for ever and it makes me feel even more like a jerk for not using a condom. It's not diseases that concern me. I've been tested and vaccinated against it all and Grace was a virgin.

I smile at her and answer her questions and kiss her, but I'm not really all there.

She even made me my favourite, pancakes, and I'm grateful. When I finished I cleaned the dishes and she suggested we take a bath.

I said "Great," but I'm now wondering if I just shouldn't tell her at all.

It would probably just worry her and it's her first time and it's supposed to be magical and hearts and flowers and it was, except for one minor slip-up on my part.

I go upstairs with her and while she gets the towels out of the linen cupboard I run the bath. I get in and it feels good. I almost begin to relax as she lays down on me with her back against my chest.

I don't want to think about the first time she was in this bath and so I decide to wash her and she takes things into her own hands and turns around and practically sits on top of my shaft, which lets me down again. I try to muster up the strength for Round Two, but I can't.

We get out and get dressed.

I drive her home. Just as she's about to get out, I note concern is showing on her face. She asks me what's wrong and I reply, "Nothing baby, I've got another night shift in a few hours, that's all."

CHAPTER NINE

Calendars

GRACE

Andrew and I have moved in together. It was all of a sudden. One minute we are at his Mum's place having the best night of my life – sex, love it. A girl's first time is so special and he was wonderful and took everything slow and I'll never, ever forget it.

He gave me a lift home and briefly kissed me goodbye and I got out of the car. He wasn't his usual self and so I didn't push him. He seemed distracted from the moment he ate breakfast, but he said it was because of work.

A week later I'm at my desk on Level 10 and I look up, as does everyone in the office, when two fine young boys in blue enter. Andrew looks so official and I can't imagine what he is doing here at this time of day.

I get up and walk up to him and he looks down at me all serious and asks quietly if he might speak to me in private.

I motion him into the Conference Room and he says, "I found us a place to live a few blocks from Mum's. Here's the address and your set of keys. I'll be moving in tomorrow with Gerry's help and if you want some help I'm off for four days from Saturday." And then he kissed me and walked away and Gerry nodded towards me and everyone's mouths opened and looked at me.

My friend Gretel asked me what happened and I told her and she said I was so lucky and dreamily looked at Gerry, who winked at her as they got into the lift. I made a mental note to invite them over to our place for our housewarming party.

Well, Andrew did move in and then on Sunday he came over to my parents' place and helped me load my meagre belongings into his car.

When I told my parents about my moving in with Andrew, they were a bit shocked. "You've been dating a few months, and less if you count your time with the therapist, take things slowly honey," said my mother.

I told them that I loved him and that I was moving out, with or without their blessing, and so on Sunday my father helped load things into Andrew's car and on our final trip they both hugged me and Dad gave Andrew the 'Don't hurt my daughter' speech.

We took a week to unpack and set everything up the way we wanted and things seemed to be going back to normal with us, but he kept watching me when he thought I wasn't looking.

I got jack of it and said, "WHAT? What is wrong? You never take your eyes off me. Am I having a bad hair day or do I have a sticker on my back, or what?" With my hands on my hips, I scowled at him. I expected an answer.

ANDREW

"I just love you so much and can't get used to the fact that you're here, living with me, and I have to keep pinching myself," I said with a genuine smile.

I hoped she would buy that, and it looked like she had when she beamed at me and started kissing me and before I knew it we were lying in bed naked and I reached over to the bedside table and ripped open the condom packet and then got her to put it on my shaft. I climbed on top of her again and without hesitation I entered her. She lets out a moan and it spurs me onward and upward. This time I'm pumping faster and faster and she's so very wet. I can feel her muscles tense and I tell her, "Come, baby," and she does, all around me, and I let go of my own need and collapse on top of her and once again it's perfect.

The morning is relaxed and we kiss and cuddle and she says she is going to take a shower. She asks me to join her, but I decline and just lie on the bed watching her naked exquisite body walk past.

I felt so lucky.

I reached behind my bedside locker and pulled out a book which I got from the library about pregnancy. It said it takes anywhere from week six to approximately week twelve before the morning sickness stops, although some get it throughout. She won't notice she's pregnant until she misses her period, and when was she due anyway? I have to ask her, but I have to be subtle.

She doesn't seem to be showing. I reflect on that and remember her beautifully taut body, which makes me horny all over again.

I put the book away when she turns off the shower and watch her come into the bedroom to get dressed. Grace asked me if I was going to stay in bed all day and rolled her eyes and laughed. I laughed too, genuinely this time. She noticed my erection and before I knew it, she's sitting on top of me and I'm in complete shock as she takes me in her mouth and I come gloriously. Grace swallows it all and sits up with a big smile on her face. I am so in love with her. I'm the luckiest man in the world. It doesn't take me long to feel the need again and this time I pull her to me as she does her hair, and she giggles and I tickle her, and once again I am removing her sweatpants and pleasuring her.

This time we both laid on the bed, spent, and had a nap. When we finally woke up it was close to 11am and my stomach is grumbling. I ask her if she is hungry and she replies, "Famished actually, don't know why. I had breakfast, a big breakfast," and she giggles some more because she means me.

I reflect on how perfectly things have turned out for us and then I begin to think back to our first time at Mum's place. It was magical for the two of us. I wish I could go back to that moment in time and put that damn condom on, and then none of this would be happening. I wouldn't be worrying every minute. We probably wouldn't have moved in together this quickly, but I'm not saying I'd change it for all the tea in China. I love waking up with Grace and having her falling asleep in my arms and the baths and everything. The only thing I would have changed was the condom.

We first had sex three weeks ago and she hasn't said she's had her period.

I go down the hall to the kitchen and tell her I'm going shopping for groceries later and ask if there's anything she wants.

Grace runs through a few things off the top of her head and I write it all down dutifully in my notebook.

"Now, let's see - Bread, Milk, Margarine, Steak, Sausages, Cheese, Salad – you decided on that, oh, and toilet paper. That should be it."

I shyly ask her what about her women's things and she tilts her head to the side and thinks. I'm waiting for the answer to all my worries.

"Gee, you're right. Stayfree Pads, they are the ones with the blue and pink wrapper but with no wings. If you're too embarrassed to get them, I can," she said.

"No, I can get all the shopping," I said smiling.

Casually I ask, "So, when are you due for your period?" and she smiles and tilts her head to the right and thinks.

"Soon," she says and kisses me and goes out the door.

I guess I just have to be patient and wait for the telltale signs of moodiness, bloating, and crying – that's always how my mother was.

"'I mean, Gretel, he actually asked me about what pads I wanted him to pick up from the shops. Most guys would have gone beetroot red."

Gretel exclaims, "You're dead right about that!"

We are going out for dinner after work. We have become firm friends and we tell each other everything. Gerry and Gretel are dating and have just started to do the "'bump and grind'" as she calls it and I say to her, "Way too much info," and we laugh hysterically as we go down in the lift.

"I think we should go to The Rocks and have Italian tonight; what do you think?" I ask Gretel, but she turns around and says, "Can we go see Gerry at the station first?"

I smile at her and say, "Sure." She's a love sick puppy.

We walk down George Street and, as we get to the police station, she turns to a mirror and does something to her hair and face and then sprays perfume on and I cough.

We go inside and at the front counter is her Gerry, but my man is nowhere to be seen. "Hey Gerry, where's Andrew?" He looks up at us and then sees Gretel and smiles. I feel like I'm intruding.

I invited them over for dinner two weeks ago and they got on very well.

"Ah, Andrew is helping the suits upstairs on a case, but I can get him if you want." I nodded and a few moments later my Mr Perfect comes into the station.

He plants a kiss on me and says, "Hello."

I love him so much and he takes my hand and looks at me all weird again.

"What?" I ask, exasperated.

"Just that you look a little tired. Are you feeling okay?" he asks.

"Yes, I just finished a long day at work and we walked here so that Juliet here could see Romeo." I smiled.

"So, what are you two up to tonight?" he asked us, changing the subject.

"Oh, just dinner and then we'll head home; you?"

"I'm working on a big case with upstairs, so I'll be a bit late," he says quietly.

"Oh, okay, I'll see you later then Andrew, I love you." I look up into his blue eyes and see that love reciprocated.

"I love you too," and he kisses me goodbye and turns around and disappears through the door.

"Gerry, how has Andrew been these last few days?" I turn my gaze onto Gerry, who looks perplexed.

"He's been a bit distracted, now that I think about it, but I thought it was this big case we're working on. There's been a lot of young women going missing around Sydney these past few months and no one can find them or the man behind it. The latest victim went missing a few blocks from here, so that's why we're working on it."

"Oh, how awful," says Gretel and she says goodbye to Gerry, giving him a big passionate kiss, and off we go to have dinner. Gerry is grinning from ear to ear.

ANDREW

Grace popped into the station and she looked tired. I accept her explanation; it is hot out there but still I've got to be extra observant, like I am at work, and I know it's going to drive her crazy, but I just can't help thinking that I'm an idiot and have probably ruined everything.

Does she look different? I don't think so. It must be that she's okay then. Am I relieved that she's not experiencing any symptoms? Yes and no, and she'd know by now if she was going to get her period, right? Girls can feel it coming on, or at least my Mum used to say so.

I have to concentrate on my work and not worry about the what-ifs, all I know is that I want to spend the rest of my life with her, and if she were to fall pregnant I would stand by her and we'd be a family.

This case I'm working on has the detectives on edge. Another woman went missing from The Rocks last week and we still haven't recovered any clues, or her body, if she's deceased.

I find working with the detectives fascinating and today I'm doing a lot of door knocking and handing out photographs of the woman to try to piece together her movements before she was reported missing by her parents.

We have also been warning young women we see out at The Rocks and Circular Quay just to be careful and not be alone after dark, as have the police at Milson's Point.

Pubs are where most of the women had been before they vanished, so we've got a few undercovers working the pubs and checking out any suspicious behaviour.

Posters have been placed around ladies' toilets and at bus stops, train stations, and restaurants. We really want to catch this person or persons.

Gerry and Gretel are getting along well I see. I would never have noticed the connection, but Grace has done a good job pairing the two up.

I should have warned both the girls to be careful and not be alone in The Rocks. I'll mention it to Grace tonight when I get home or before she leaves for work.

GRACE

Calendars are for keeping track of important dates such as birthdays, wedding anniversaries, and the like, but mine keeps track of my cycle too.

I go to my mobile phone and open up my calendar of events and check it. I saw the pads Andrew left for me on our bed when I got home and that jogged my memory.

It was so good of him to go buy them for me. He is a rare find, for sure. I scroll through the months to find February and work back from there.

Hmm, I had my last period five weeks ago!

I'm late. It's probably because of moving out. I mean, leaving home for the first time is pretty scary, even if you are moving in with the man of your dreams.

I go into the bathroom and have my bath with the nice smelly bath bombs that Andrew likes. When I got out, I went to the long mirror in the bedroom and turned myself around and around wondering if I'd gotten bigger in the lower belly, like I do when expecting my period.

I had my normal sore boobs and was a little tired, but no moodiness or even cramps. What was going on? And then I remembered my mother saying that sometimes the moon and your own body aligns and you may be late due to that. Plus being in close proximity to the women at work will in fact affect your cycle, so that was probably it. Good.

I wasn't worried about anything else. My job was sometimes stressful, especially when my boss was ordering me around because she had flown into the office saying she had a conference in fifteen minutes and requires the boardroom to be set up, which usually means glasses and a decanter full of icy cold water.

Photocopies of whatever she throws at me, and all in place before the CEO or whomever she is meeting with, arrives.

When she's interstate I relax a little, but of course I get work directed at me via emails and fax from wherever she is at any time.

I'm proficient and efficient and she has yet to find fault in my work. I really love my job, although this week I've been a bit lacking in gusto. It was noted by her because she always expects me to be at the top of my game.

ANDREW

I'm beat. I was going to talk to Grace about what's happening at work, but she's passed out on our bed and so I shower and climb in beside her. I instinctively hold her with my right arm around her middle, but lately I've been aiming lower and she squirms beside me as I nuzzle her neck. I'm too tired to fool around and so within moments I'm asleep.

In the morning I woke up before Grace, which is highly unusual and so I look at the alarm clock and realise that if she doesn't get up now, she'll be late.

I kiss her cheek and gently say, "Wakey, wakey". Grace stirs in my arms and opens up her eyes and closes them again under the glare from the windows. "It's Friday, baby, but you still have to go to work today."

Grace stretches and then looks at me and down at my hand, which is still resting on her belly. I swallow and move my hand away. She looks at me again and then gets up.

I get up with her and we go to the kitchen and have breakfast. Grace has a boiled egg every morning and so I start to boil two eggs and she puts on the toast. When we sit down, she sniffs the egg and asks me if it smells off, and I sniff it and say, "No."

I go to the sink after eating and clean up our plates. I tell her I'm going to have a shower as I'm on day shift for the time being. Grace nods.

She looks a little pale. Grace heads to the bedroom and begins to get out her clothes for work.

GRACE

It's now six weeks since I last got my periods. I should have been on the pill. I'll go to the doctor and get a prescription today. Worrying about not getting it is often the reason you don't get it.

That egg for breakfast is not sitting well on my stomach at all. It must have been off. Perhaps Andrew has a blocked nose?

I have my shower after Andrew and get dressed and he drives me to the station. I kiss him on the lips and I get out and he finds parking. We get the train into work together. I read and he goes over his 'contemporaneous notes.'

At about 11.30am he phones me on my mobile and asks if I want to catch up for lunch, but I tell him I'm working through as I have a deadline, and he believes me. I leave the building and head to the medical centre in Pitt Street.

I wait nervously to see the female doctor. When finally I am called inside, she asks me what the problem is and I nervously explain that I've not had my period.

"It has been six weeks since I last bled," I say.

"Are you sexually active?" she asks.

"I live with my boyfriend and so, yes, I am sexually active," I reply. She asks, "Have you ever had a pap smear?"

I say, "No, I only just started to have sex six weeks ago. I've been through a lot lately and I guess that's why I'm late." I told her about what I'd been through and she nods and says, "That can sometimes be the cause of you not menstruating but," she continues, "do you use condoms or are you on the pill?"

"My boyfriend uses condoms," I say.

"That's why I came to see you. I want to go on the pill," I mutter.

"Well, we'll have to do a pregnancy test on you first." She sends me to a pathologist and I go. I hate needles. I can't be pregnant.

He uses condoms and I know they haven't ruptured. I've seen them. It must be the moon or something else, like a tummy bug or, as the doctor said, stress.

CHAPTER TEN

Just a Bug

ANDREW

It's odd that Grace said no to having lunch with me. We usually have lunch on Fridays, but she sounded distracted so I didn't push.

When I got home that night Grace was making dinner and smiled at me and I smiled back. I went to have a shower and, just as dinner was ready, I emerged from the bedroom.

She didn't speak much while we ate.

"What's wrong Grace? You're so quiet, did something happen at work?" I ask her with concern.

"Nothing, it's all okay. I'm just tired. I'm going to go to bed early tonight, if that's okay?" she says.

"Sure, you sure you're okay?"

"Yep," she says.

After dinner she goes and has a bath and slips into bed.

I'm cleaning the kitchen and decide to watch TV.

Something is wrong. Perhaps she got her period and she's just moody and tired. I relax.

I sit at my computer and read a few of my emails and type up some reports for work until I feel tired enough to sleep.

It's unusual for Grace to go to bed any time before 8.30pm, but as I walk down the hallway there she is in our bed fast asleep, her chest rising and falling deeply, and she has shadows under her eyes and I move closer to her and kneel beside her and just watch her.

How I love her so. With every breath I breathe my love grows and I know she is my future. How lucky I am to have her in my life.

If she is pregnant, I'll be there for her. I'd love her so much and we'd be happy and so I crawl into bed and wrap my arm around her and rest my hand once again on her lower belly and note it feels the same as always.

I stroke it, hoping that it will help with her cramps. Mum always said Dad used to do that and it made her relax more.

I kissed her shoulder and laid my head beside hers on the pillow and dreamt of her.

GRACE

I got up and went to the bathroom and had to throw up. I was hoping that Andrew wouldn't hear me. I flushed and then I cleaned my face and brushed my teeth and strolled down to the kitchen and Andrew was making me breakfast. He stopped and looked at me.

"Grace, are you feeling okay? You look pale. Do you want to sit down here or stay in bed? I can give you your eggs in bed. I'll ring your work if you want to stay home."

I look at the plate. Eggs again, only scrambled this time. I take one whiff of them and say, "Sorry," and I run to the toilet and throw up again.

Andrew followed me and kept the door open as I knelt down on the bathroom floor with my head in the toilet bowl. I didn't even register he was there until I felt his hands on my back and lifting my hair out of the way. My stomach was squeezing out its contents, time and time again. He hovered.

When I had finished throwing up, he gave me a face cloth and I wiped my mouth and face, feeling the refreshing cold water. I felt I was burning up.

"What's wrong? Are you sick?" He looked into my eyes and he was very worried.

I motioned that I wanted up. He stood and pulled me up into his arms and I said, "Thanks."

He let me go and I walked into the bedroom to get my stuff out for work. "Aren't you going to eat your breakfast? You really should eat something," he said.

The thought of eating made me feel squeamish again and I shook my head. I stood still for a few seconds deciding if I should go back into the bathroom and I took a step to do that, but a wave of dizziness takes me. Andrew grabs me and holds me up.

"I've got a tummy bug or something. It'll pass. I feel much better now," and in fact I did.

He looked at me for a long time and then went to the kitchen. He drove me to the station.

At lunchtime I was at the kitchen table and I just couldn't eat my egg, lettuce, and tomato sandwich with mayo which Gretel had gotten me, one of my favourites. We sat in the lunch room and I felt woozy again.

I got up to get a drink of water and felt the room spin – violently. Not like this morning.

The next thing I know is that Andrew is kneeling over me and is ready to burst with concern. I blink once, twice, and realise I'm on a couch in my boss's office.

"What happened?" I ask.

"You got up from the table and then fainted. You hit your head on the floor pretty bad and I was going to call an ambulance. I didn't know what to do, so I called Andrew, who was on his way here anyway, and he got here really quickly," said Gretel.

I looked at Andrew and smiled. I wanted to sit up. He helped me and the world swam again, and I felt like I was going to throw up. I groaned and lay back down.

"You're not feeling well, Grace. I'll take you home," he said softly, feeling my forehead.

He picked me up and carried me to a taxi and we went directly to his Mum's home. She was away and we were housesitting every second night to give the impression that someone was still living there.

When we got inside, he sat me down on the couch and put a blanket over my legs and got me a lemonade with water added and watched me like a hawk. All I wanted was a bucket.

I got the courage from somewhere and so I told him, expecting him to yell at me.

"I'm late," I said.

"Late for what, baby?" says Andrew

"I was wanting to go on the pill because I realised I was late and the doctor wanted me to have a pregnancy test first. It's just a precaution, but you've always used a condom Andrew, so I think it's just the moon or something."

"Did you contact the doctor to find out if you were pregnant?" he said with a tremor in his voice.

"No, I forgot," I say guiltily.

"Give me the number," Andrew asked and then he phones the surgery. He gives the handset to me and I feel faint. "Hello, this is Grace O'Malley, yes, results." I look up at Andrew and he looks at me with such intensity that I get scared and tears well in my eyes.

"Grace, you're not pregnant, but you do have a bacterial infection and gastroenteritis. I think bed rest is what is needed and if your boyfriend could swing past the surgery I'll write you a prescription for the pill and your antibiotics," says my doctor.

"Thanks."

"Well, what did she say?" he asks.

"Negative, but I do have a bad case of something. I'm going to bed. Can you go get my prescriptions and then go to the chemist and get them filled?"

He nods. I rattled off the address of the surgery.

I get up from the couch and walk out of the room. Andrew gets up.

I walk up the stairs and as I get towards the top I begin to feel like shit. Somebody just kill me!

I'm standing with my back to the stairs as I reach the top landing.

I place my foot on the edge of the top step, unaware of anything. I begin to lean forward to take the final step. My head swims and I feel myself free-falling and I can't grip the banister, which seems to be running away from me.

My foot leaves the step and I'm now almost horizontal with the stairs and my eyes close. It's slow motion.

Oh, help me!

I feel weightless and my stomach drops.

ANDREW

I'm so in love with Grace that I actually start thinking about our future.

I went to the jewellery store and I looked at a ring which I know she'll love. I will give it to her tonight. I want to spend the rest of my life with her. I also start thinking about maybe getting a place of our own because I hate renting.

I'm coming back from the store and my mobile phone goes off and it's Gretel.

"Hey Gretel, what's up?" I ask, feeling very cheerful.

"Andrew, it's Grace, I think you'd better come over here, she fainted and hit her head and she looks just awful. I was going to call for an ambulance, but I don't know what to do," she says, rather upset.

I tell her I'll be there in five minutes, and I was. I get to the foyer and press the button to take me up to the tenth floor and when I get there I see Gretel in Grace's boss' office, with Grace sprawled out on the couch looking pale.

Grace stirs and asks what happened. Gretel tells her.

Grace looks at me and smiles tentatively and tries to sit up, but she grows even more pale and I can tell she's not well and I pick her up and take her to Mum's place; she's away and we're house sitting. I lay her on the couch and put a blanket over her. I sit with her. I get her a lemonade and she sips it.

Grace says, "I'm late."

I'm a little confused and enquire, "Late for what, baby?"

Grace looks down and says, "I was wanting to go on the pill and because I was late and the doctor wanted me to have a pregnancy test first. It's just a precaution, but you've always used a condom Andrew, so I just think it's the moon or something."

"Did you contact the doctor to find out if you were pregnant?"

"No, I forgot," she says.

I get the telephone and dial her doctor. I hand it to her and wait. After she hangs up, she gets up and tears are in her eyes. I get up, not sure what she's going to say or do. Why doesn't she tell me? The suspense is killing me.

"Well, what did she say?" I ask.

"Negative, but I do have a bad case of something. I'm going to bed."

She asks me to get her prescriptions and get them filled and I nod that I will.

Grace mounts the steps and walks up to the top floor. I watch her intently.

She looks exhausted. I walk to the edge of the hall.

As Grace reaches the second step from the top, she stops. Her hand absentmindedly goes to her mouth and she takes the last step and my life flashes before my eyes as she falls towards me. Her left hand reaches out towards the banister but misses it, and her feet lose contact with the stairs.

I don't know how I managed to cross the floor and get to the stairs before she hit them, but I did.

I'm on my knees holding her head up and her body is crashing down onto me and I slide further down, with her legs limp and her behind whacking the bottom steps.

I lay her down on the floor in the hallway, panting and worried.

She's out cold.

I place my hand on her neck and her pulse is still going.

I start feeling her head and arms and legs for anything broken, but she seems to be intact. I carry her up to our bed and lay her down.

I lie next to her and wait for her to wake up. I should call an ambulance so once the shock wears off I go to get the phone, but I don't want to leave her.

She wakes up and groans.

Grace looks at me and cries.

"Hey baby, what's with the tears? C'mon, tell me, you can talk to me honey, please?"

"I'm not pregnant." Her voice is flat and she turns over onto her side, away from me.

I roll her towards me and she's crying more heavily.

I hold her to my chest and tell her, "It's okay," but part of me is confused. She seems sad that she's not pregnant, but... "Grace, look at me."

She raises her tear-stained eyes to me.

"I forgot to put on a condom. It was your first time. I forgot. I thought you might be pregnant but you're not, so we have all the time in the world for that. Someday in the future. Why are you crying, baby answer me?"

She turns around and vomits on the floor. "I'm sorry for the mess." She sinks into the mattress and groans.

"It doesn't change anything. I still love you," I say and get up to get a bucket and a mop. Thank God we have wooden floors.

There would be time enough for me to give her the ring. Right now, though, she needs fluids and I'll go get her prescription and get it filled once she nods off.

GRACE

I wake up and I'm in Andrew's old room. I moan as pain floods me. I open my eyes to find Andrew anxiously sitting next to me. He hands me a glass of water and the antibiotics plus some pain killers. He told my doctor what happened, no doubt.

I swallow them dutifully and then he hands me a bowl of chicken soup. He feeds me like a baby.

I feel better.

He looks exhausted and concern is showing on his face and his eyes never leave mine.

"What?" I ask.

"Did you think you might be pregnant, Grace?" he asks.

"Yes, I did for a few days 'cause the doctor wanted me to have a test," I tell him.

"Did you want to be pregnant, Grace?" he asks.

"No, yes, no! I don't know. It happened all too fast. We've only just started living together and I didn't want to ruin what we have. I was terrified to tell you," I said, tears welling in my eyes.

He places his hand on my cheek and rubs his thumb to wipe away the tears that have escaped.

"If you had been pregnant, it wouldn't have been your fault, Grace. I was the one who forgot to wear a condom, not you. I should have told you that very day, but I was scared too and as the weeks wore on I started to think that you might be.

I had no way of telling when your period was due, so I came up with the ruse of going shopping and picking up your pads."

"Oh." I smile.

"I realised that if you were pregnant that I'd stand by you no matter what. We'd get our own place, not rent anymore, and we'd be a family."

"I, I want to do something now, so please stay quiet as it is something I have thought about for a while now and I need to concentrate."

He got up off the bed and opened up the box in front of me and there was a ring inside. It was beautiful.

"Grace, you are the one, most precious and beloved woman I could ever know and I want to spend the rest of my life with you, please say you'll do me the greatest honour and say yes."

I swallow.

I looked at him in utter shock and quietly said, "Yes."

He kissed me and hugged me and loved me. Right there and then I was the happiest woman alive.

ANDREW

We head down to the lounge room and my mother barges through the front door and looks a little shocked to see us there. We tell her our news and she's so happy for us and insists we celebrate. I get us a lemonade and she looks at us and says, "NO, champagne, darling. You're getting married. Oh, you look so happy."

I look at Grace and we stand in front of my mother. I hand Grace a lemonade. I say, "Sit down mum. Grace has gastro or something."

My mother mouths "Oh, perhaps champagne can wait till later, you don't look that well dear. Perhaps I should get you something to eat. Oh, I can't believe you're getting married. I've got so many people to phone, have you set a date yet?"

Grace says, for no apparent reason, "As long as it's not eggs," and smiles at me and then at my mother, who is now crying happily in the background. I notice a sudden change in Grace's face and then she faints.

I caught her head just as it was about to hit the coffee table and I laid her on the couch with her feet up in the air.

My mother hovered and fanned her face. Grace came to a short while later and looked rather green in the face.

She sat up slowly and asked for a bucket.

My mother went to the laundry to get one and, as she placed it at her feet, Grace vomited again.

My mother said, "Poor baby, she's not pregnant is she?"

I look at her with a face, partly annoyed, and she says, "I'll get her some tea; it will settle her stomach."

I rubbed her back as I held her hair out from her face again. I was worried. Could the blood test be wrong?

Grace sat back and I wiped her mouth and face again with a cold cloth and she smiled weakly.

"I'm suddenly really tired. Can I have a nap upstairs?"

"Sure, you know where it is," I said.

"Thanks," she said.

I mustn't have been thinking clearly, because I would normally be hovering over her after what had happened earlier on the stairs. It wasn't until she got to the bottom that I realised and got up.

She stood and turned around and said, "Oh no," and collapsed onto the floor.

I picked her up and took her to bed. I stayed with her until morning. She seemed better. I woke her up in the middle of the night to take her next antibiotic and now she was due another one.

CHAPTER ELEVEN

Surprises

GRACE

Will I ever stop throwing up?

I get up to go upstairs and the next thing I know I'm lying in bed next to Andrew and he is asking me to take my antibiotic, and then again this morning. I feel better. I note when I went to the bathroom that I have spots in my underwear. I start to take my pill.

After a fortnight on the pill, Andrew and I are like rabbits. It's good now, we are more relaxed and Andrew loves not having to wear a condom. I do too and it feels so much better. My senses are heightened.

I didn't get a full-on period, but I think I read somewhere that that's normal when starting to take the pill, plus I was sick with gastro-something.

I've been on the pill now for six weeks. Gretel convinces me to go to the doctor again as I'm not looking well again. It's now 12.30pm.

"You might need another course of antibiotics." She comes with me.

It's a different doctor and she writes me up another prescription after I explain my symptoms. Gretel is waiting impatiently for me in the waiting room and takes my hand when I sit down in the seat next to her. I tell her that I'm going to go home and she says she'll tell my boss.

I telephoned Andrew to advise I was going home sick instead of hanging out with Gretel to go see a movie and he was worried again and said he'd be sleeping all afternoon as he was on night shift. I was going to get a taxi, so he seemed okay with that because I think he wanted to come and get me.

When I got home, Andrew was at the front door with that concerned look on his face. I kissed him and just had some lemonade and watched TV and he went to have a sleep. I went to bed at 9pm just as he was getting up to shower and head to work.

That night I couldn't sleep. Andrew was on night shift. All I could manage was nanna naps and, broken sleep and I felt exhausted.

I woke up after dozing at 5.30am. I got a train into the city with the thought of seeing him, but I got as far as the corner of his building in George Street and almost walked inside but couldn't because another wave of nausea hit me, so I went for a walk and sat on the wall where I had first seen Andrew. The early morning light was on the harbour as the GPO clock chimed seven in the distance. I hugged my knees to myself and watched the harbour come alive. Andrew was finishing work.

ANDREW

I turn up at home and there's a note from Grace telling me she couldn't sleep and was coming to the city to see me, but she didn't turn up.

Where the hell is she? I paced the floor, getting angry, worried, and scared.

I phoned Gretel and she hadn't seen her since the doctor's.

Now she's sick again. Where the hell is she?

I was frantic.

I decided to go to work and put out an unofficial missing person report. Perhaps my fellow police officers out there would find her and I could get her home.

I get to work and do just that and was assured 'unofficially' that all would be done to find her. It hasn't been long enough to report her as actually missing, so it's the best we can do. I'm off duty but I can't go home. Gerry turns up to see if he can help.

Gerry and I walk our beat. I'm looking everywhere, expecting to see her.

As we approach the Sydney Harbour Bridge, Gerry nudges my arm and nods in the direction of the wall where I first saw Grace, and sure enough she's there.

I run up to her and Gerry's not too far behind me.

I wrap her up in my arms and ask her why she's here. "It's not safe for you to be here on your own. Grace, I was so worried." I hug her again and kiss her head.

"I felt sick. I needed fresh air and I like it here. I can think. Sorry for worrying you again."

"It's alright now, you're safe," I said.

"I'm going to go now anyway and go to work, it's a bit early, but I've missed a lot of work of late," she said.

"No, you're not up to it," I plead. "You look sick, Grace."

"Andrew, I've thrown up three times this morning and I'm hungry."

"What's wrong, you should be over the gastro-something. Did you go get another course of antibiotics?"

Grace looks past me at Gerry and then at me. Gerry smiles shyly and walks down the hill a bit and radios to the station that Grace has been found alive and well.

"I'm sorry, Andrew."

"For what?" he says.

"I'm still sick. Yes, the doctor gave me more antibiotics."

"Hey, it's okay. I've heard it's going around, some of the guys at the station are off with it, so don't apologise. You never have to apologise to me. I wanted to know you were okay. Those missing women… if something happened to you, I'd just die, so please from now on don't be in this area on your own promise me."

She promised.

"We'll go get you a tea to help settle your stomach and get some food into you," I say.

She nods.

As Grace stands up, she swallows hard and for a second I think she's going to pass out or throw up.

"Andrew, could you carry me? I don't think my legs are working." She smiles up at me.

I scoop her up into my arms and take her to the station. She feels so light, she's lost too much weight, and I sit her down in the tea room. Sipping her tea, she starts to look better. I give her some cereal and she keeps each tentative swallow down.

I drive her to her office. I'd rather take her home, but I don't want to argue with her.

I phone her each hour and check that she is okay.

I met her for lunch and we just talked about what we were going to do on the weekend. If Grace was up to it, I wanted to go wedding venue hunting.

After work, I picked her up and we drove home.

We had a quiet night and watched television and she had a bath and went to bed early. I followed her after a while and slept until the next morning. She had to take the pill and the antibiotic as soon as she woke up.

I heard her throwing up in the bathroom after breakfast.

I think I might have to take her to the doctor. This bug is going to kill her, and me, if she doesn't stop throwing up.

I was worrying about her all the time and I didn't tell her this, but it was affecting my work and my Captain was concerned for both of us.

I had to stop thinking about her when I got to work, or I'd be a mess and out of a job.

GRACE

I don't understand it, I wake up each morning and I feel sick. Could it be gastro-something… still? I look in the mirror and I look awful. I have shadows beneath my eyes and I've lost weight. I've not seen much of Andrew this past fortnight because he is on night shift, and I'm going out the door just as he comes home.

He's also working on that case about the missing women. We haven't made love for ages and I miss him.

I have my breakfast of dry toast and tea (I've gone off coffee too now) and get dressed and, just as I'm leaving, Andrew comes home. I wonder if he's avoiding me?

Maybe he doesn't love me anymore or doesn't want to get married? But he stops in the vestibule and really sees me for the first time in days and he has that concerned look on his face. He touches my cheek with his palm. I look up at him and I kiss him with all the love I feel for him. I taste him and I yearn for him.

He senses that and drops his coat and bag and walks me towards the kitchen table and, before I know it, he is inside me again. I'm so happy. He needs me. When we are finished, he pulls out of me and I ask him if he is okay.

He tells me he's okay.

He holds me close and tells me he's missed me and he loves me. I feel the same. He promises to cut back on his hours and spend more time with me. I like that thought.

He looks at me again and says, "You've been sick again? Are you feeling okay? You have lost so much weight and you don't look at all well."

"I'm feeling better." I don't know how long this will last, but each week I'm feeling a little better.

"You look exhausted, go to bed Andrew. I'll see you tonight."

"Yep, I'm definitely that. But I'm back to day shift tomorrow." He kisses me and walks towards our bedroom.

I go to work.

On Friday afternoon, at work I began to feel off again. It was noted. My boss told me to go home.

Gretel and I are now at The Rocks looking out over the harbour. I needed to get some air because I was feeling sick again, so I walked to the Sydney Harbour Bridge with the intention of going home with Andrew. I was taking deep breaths to still the rising sick feeling and dizziness. It was 3pm.

Gretel gets out her mobile phone and phones someone. She walks away from me so I can't hear her conversation. It's most probably Gerry. I grin thinking about how well they are getting on and I know she's worried about me, but I've not fainted for a week now, so things are looking up.

"Hey Gerry, Grace and I are underneath the Sydney Harbour Bridge. Can you get yourself and Andrew down here pretty soon? I think Grace is going to need some TLC and a bucket or an ambulance. She's thrown up five times since we left the office and can barely stand up."

"Who were you talking to?" I ask.

"Who? Me? Only a friend. I happen to know lots of people apart from you." She smiles but seems distracted and looks behind us.

While we are standing there, leaning against the railing with my head facing down as another wave of nausea and dizziness over takes me, Gretel comments that the weather is getting colder.

She drapes her cardigan over my shoulders and stands next to me, but with her back to the harbour.

"I think I made the wrong choice," I said.

"What choice?" she asks.

"I should have gone home first and waited for Andrew there. I'm feeling worse now," I said.

I had to change my attitude and be perky and happy when I got to his office. He was worried about me and I know it must be affecting his work.

The very last thing I want and need is for him to worry about me too much and get stressed, and I would hate it if my illness was the cause of him losing his job.

I would rather leave him than have that happen.

ANDREW

Gretel phoned Gerry and he told me what she said. I nodded to him silently and we left the station and drove towards the Harbour Bridge. When we got there, a crowd was forming and Gretel was crying. When she saw Gerry, she raced over to him and cried into his chest.

I walked through the crowd and Gerry tried to disperse them, saying we needed room and slowly, one by one, they began to move away.

There were comments in the air like "She's dead" and "Look at the colour of her skin."

I knelt down beside her and gingerly felt the pulse in her neck, and it was slow but very much there.

I hadn't realised I'd stopped breathing myself and so I took a deep breath and gently tapped her cheek to try to wake her up.

Gerry got onto his radio and requested an ambulance.

"Hey, Grace, wake up," I said to her, right near her ear.

Nothing.

I felt her forehead and asked the crowd to allow room for the ambulance that was on its way.

When the ambos arrived, I told them all I could and Gretel filled them in and they rubbed Grace's sternum to rouse her and then put her on a gurney and inside the ambulance, away from spectators, they put her on oxygen and examined her.

I told the female paramedic I was her fiancé. They passed a foul-smelling bottle under her nose and before long had Grace sitting up and conscious, if a bit listless.

One paramedic stayed in the back with us while her partner drove and she smiled at Grace and I held her hand. A few minutes into the journey, she motioned to us that she was going to be sick. The paramedic gave her a bag and sure enough she vomited and when she finished she groaned.

I was so relieved that she was awake and breathing normally and that slowly her colouring was coming back.

The paramedic asked her lots of questions about past illnesses and smiled and was really nice, and we even got talking about rugby. I didn't follow rugby, but it kept my mind busy instead of worrying about Grace. I knew what she was trying to do. I was grateful, but nothing could ever really make me not worry about Grace.

When we got to the hospital, she was ushered into the Emergency Ward and they examined her and took blood.

It was several hours later that they told me what was wrong.

Grace was pregnant. I couldn't wait to tell her, but when I went to her room she was sleeping. She was exhausted from all the trauma her body had gone through and they had given her something to settle her stomach.

CHAPTER TWELVE

Future Things

GRACE

'Where am I? This place doesn't look familiar to me, and where is Andrew and what are all these tubes doing in me?'

I'm wearing a white hospital gown, but I am naked underneath and I'm in pain everywhere.

I hear low voices behind the curtain and I need water. "Hello, (my voice raspy) is Andrew there?" I say, oh so quietly, as a face appears in front of me and smiles through the haze.

"Do you want some water, baby?" asks Andrew, and I nod.

Little shards of ice trickle down my throat and I smile at how wonderful it tastes, and then he takes it away and I smile up at him but fade off into sleep once more.

When I woke up much later, it must have been in the dead of night that I realised I had to pee. Andrew was leaning on my bed with his head resting on my leg. He was exhausted.

I decided the need to pee was more important than anything, so I slowly raised myself on my elbows and eased my leg from under his head. Oh so slowly, I moved my left leg.

As I was about to throw back the sheets, a hand grabbed my arm from behind me. I turned around out of fear but it was Andrew. "What are you doing? Where are you going? You're supposed to stay in bed," he whispered.

"I have to go to the bathroom," I say to him.

He walks around to my side of the bed and carries me to the bathroom and puts me down gently and I ask him to go outside. He looks at me as if he is about to say, "No way," but agrees to turn around at least and give me some privacy.

I sat there and let it all go. It felt marvellous and when I'd finished I stood up with his help. He flushed the toilet and I washed my hands, whilst he stood behind me holding me up.

He carried me back into bed.

ANDREW

"What are you doing? Where are you going? You're supposed to be in bed."

When Grace looked at me, I saw fear in her eyes for a second and so I walked around towards her because she told me she had to use the bathroom.

I picked her up and deposited her in there, but I was not leaving her, not for a second. Her blood pressure was still low and she would likely faint again.

I eventually turned around and let her have some privacy.

When she finished, I helped her up, carried her back to bed. I was so relieved she'd woken up and was okay. Grace fell asleep again but woke up in time for breakfast, and she was starving.

"Now that you are on the mend, I might be able to take you home tomorrow. You've been here for two days already and it's high time we slept together in our bed in our own room. Hospital chairs aren't the most comfortable beds, but I've slept in worse," and she smiles at me.

"You'll have to take things easy for a while and rest, lots of rest." I paused and then continued, "By the way, our baby is doing fine too." I smiled that big smile that I reserve for her and only her.

"Baby?"

"Grace, you're pregnant." I smiled and nodded.

"So, the gastric-something wasn't gastric-something second time round... I was actually pregnant? How? I was on the pill," I said.

154

"Grace, the doctor here said that, when you are on the pill and you go on antibiotics, you should take extra precautions. We didn't and now we're pregnant." I smiled at her and squeezed her hand.

I was so happy to have her back and, as for the baby subject, we could discuss that at a later time when she was feeling stronger, but for now she ate her breakfast with fervour and then promptly fell asleep again.

****

ANDREW

Well, I finally got her to say, "I do," and we are at home relaxing before the impending birth of our baby in another few weeks. We decided to not have a honeymoon as we need all the money we earn to buy our own place one day soon. She's getting so big. In the meantime, we are staying at my mother's while she's away again.

I turn to her and tell her I love her at every opportunity, and I tell her how beautiful she is to me and I cuddle her and rub her baby belly often and read to him or her and sing so that I can be a part of its life even before it's born. Grace laughs at me.

I go maternity-dress shopping with her and we go to baby shops and read up on everything concerning babies, birth, and child-rearing and our mothers are hovering, which is to be expected.

We chose a cot and have umpteen bags of diapers and hand-me-downs from friends and family and we are pretty close to having everything ready for the day we bring our little bundle of joy into this world.

At night I watch Grace as she sleeps and I put my hands on her extended belly and feel the baby moving, kicking, and once I thought it had the hiccups, which made me laugh. I was so looking forward to being a father, now that I'd gotten over the shock.

Grace is going to make a wonderful mother and she's strong and emotionally ready for this huge change in our lives.

I am in awe of her.

GRACE

I went to bed early whilst Andrew was talking to his mother on the phone and he sounded so proud and was telling her about all our plans and renovations, and that since we were having a baby after all, that we'd need to use her room, but she apparently didn't mind. He was only pulling her leg and they laugh.

I got up for the bathroom a short time later and, as I was on the toilet, I felt a sharp stabbing pain in my belly, then another, and then one that made my breath catch in my throat. Was it the baby kicking or Braxton-Hicks or the real thing? I'd been having false labour pains for a while but these were beginning to really hurt.

I got up and found myself dizzy again and put my hand out to the towel rack and pain overtook me and I bent over gasping.

I heard Andrew downstairs watching TV whilst he was on the phone, to Gerry now.

I staggered to the top of the stairs and tried to make my way down towards him.

A contraction came on and it felt like glass ripping through my middle. I screamed and collapsed onto my knees.

Andrew stops his conversation and listens, but by then I'm panting to catch my breath and he goes back to his conversation.

I crawl toward the nursery and lean up to the baby monitor and turn it on. The downstairs monitor is on the coffee table and I call out to him in the middle of the contraction. I feel my stomach and it feels like a wave at the beach rippling through me and with each contraction my hips stretch further apart.

I hear him at the other end of the monitor saying, "Hmm… the baby monitor just turned itself on."

I cry out loud, begging him to come as my water breaks around me.

Within seconds he's on the floor with me, by my side.

He feels the water on the floor and rubs my back and tells me it will be okay. He calls an ambulance.

He carries me to the bedroom.

ANDREW

I'm on the phone to Gerry and we're talking about the case and I see the light of the baby monitor go on, which is strange. I listen but I can't hear anything, so I keep chatting. Then I hear Grace scream and cry out my name and I'm up the stairs and in the nursery within thirty seconds.

I find her on her knees surrounded by water. Her waters have broken. I call for an ambulance. I get onto the ambulance dispatch centre and they walk me through how to check how far she is along and I advise she is dilated about eight centimetres and they tell me to prepare for delivery and that an ambulance will be along as soon as possible. I carry her to our bed.

I go to the linen cupboard and get clean towels and sheets and scissors and thread and hold her hand as she goes through contraction after contraction. This baby is not going to wait.

I set her up, ready to deliver our baby, and I laid the towels in between her legs and told her that I could see the baby's head. One final push was all that was required, said the dispatcher, and sure enough out came our baby boy just as I heard an ambulance approach.

I cut the cord and wrap him up in a blanket and hand him to Grace, and we are in love with him already. The ambulance officers let themselves in and immediately begin to check Grace out and get the baby cleaned up. They bundled them off to the hospital in the ambulance and I rode in the front with the driver. I couldn't wipe the smile off my face.

When Grace was settled into her bed and our little bundle was beside us in his crib, I stopped and looked at my son and my wife. I loved them both dearly.

I stayed up all night looking at my son and I felt so much love pouring out of me, and when our parents arrived the next morning, I felt so proud and Grace was much better and was out of bed. Soon enough we would be going home.

When they all left, I turned to Grace and said, "I'll say it again, I'm the luckiest man on this earth," as I looked down at my wife and our son. Grace said, "Yes, you are, Mr Perfect."

SOMETHING EXTRA

ANDREW

It was a lazy spring day and Grace and I were in the back yard while our son was asleep in his crib next to us.

I asked her something that I had pushed into the back of my mind.

"Grace, was it you who sat on a busy train one day and a police officer sat beside you and held your hand?"

Grace nearly choked on her biscuit.

So, it truly was her and I smiled. I had not really put two and two together. What were the odds?

"Oh My God! That was you! I wanted you to take me to my formal. That was why I was in the city. I had to buy a dress, and oh!" she said.

"What?" I asked.

"Your mother was the woman who sold me my dress!"

I couldn't believe it.

"Grace, we are so meant to be together."

She nodded and we glanced over at our son and smiled as I reached over to hold her hand.

"I kicked myself for not giving you my phone number," I said.

"Same," and she laughed.

I found myself laughing too.

If a person tells me there is no such thing as love at first sight, I will tell them they are wrong because from the moment I laid eyes on Grace, I was gone!

The End

www.ingramcontent.com/pod-product-compliance
Lightning Source LLC
Chambersburg PA
CBHW071720140626
46557CB00012B/982